ALSO BY MICHAEL NEWTON

GIDEON THORN

Skinwalker

LEVIATHAN RISING

LEVIATHAN RISING

GIDEON THORN
BOOK 2

MICHAEL NEWTON

LEVIATHAN RISING

PROLOGUE

CHIHUAHUAN DESERT, WEST TEXAS

The Mexicans and Chinese didn't get along. Seely Ridpath, foreman of the Belle Aire Mine, was conscious of the boss man's plan in that regard for keeping wages low, both sides uneasy about having men replaced if they made any trouble, but it still caused problems on the job.

Language was part of it. The two groups only managed to communicate as far as both could manage some version of garbled English, typically salted with words in Spanish or Cantonese that went over the listeners' heads. Ridpath himself spoke neither foreign tongue adeptly, but could hold his own in simple Spanish and was picking up a little of the pidgin jabbered by celestials. For anything related to the mine and its security, he'd ordered all concerned to learn the proper English terms in order to enlighten him posthaste.

Another thing was attitude. Both races were hard workers for the most part, fewer slackers than he'd have expected using local white boys or the Cornish diggers at the Silver Crown nearby. Still, they were at odds on things like holidays, the Mexicans expecting Sunday mornings off for Mass and sundry saint's days, while the Chinese pitched in seven days a week without complaint, claiming the over-time while Mexicans went off to be with God. Ridpath would happily have put his foot down on the mumbo-jumbo, but his boss approved it as a sideways kind of Christianity and let it go.

As far as food went, everyone ate pork and beans with biscuits on the site or brought their own in dinner pails, whatever was the going fare along Celestial Alley in New Egypt, or in camp outside of town where all the Mexicans bunked down. Ridpath was satisfied to eat free on the boss man's dime and had his own shack at the mine and spent most of his time there, eyes peeled for the kind of trouble that was always rife around a mining claim, sneak thieves and union organizers for the most part.

Underground and on their meal breaks, he could feel the Mexicans and Chinese chafing on each other in a lot of ways. They muttered insults at each other in their native tongues, incomprehensible but spoken with a tone only an idiot would fail to understand, then swore to Ridpath's face that they were only making small talk with their fellow countrymen. At other times—say if a Chinaman required some tool the Mexicans were using or vice versa, and they didn't have a spare—the party with the object would pretend he couldn't understand the simplest of requests and hold things up until Ridpath appeared to rage at everyone, demanding that they work together or ship out.

Near dusk today, though, when a clutch of miners poured out of the adit calling Ridpath's name, they seemed to have a single thought in mind. He couldn't understand what they were telling him at first, and had to make them slow it down.

"*Una caverna*," said the chosen spokesman for the troubled-looking Mexicans.

"How's that?" Ridpath inquired.

"*Dòngxué*," declared a miner Ridpath took to be the head celestial.

"English!" the foreman snapped. Then louder, as if all of them were deaf, "ENGLISH!"

"A cavern," said the mouthpiece for the Mexicans, raising his voice to match Ridpath's.

"A *what?*"

"Caven," the Chinese spokesman said, doing his best.

Now Ridpath understood them, but that didn't mean he was believing it. "Show me."

They led him into darkness, smoky lanterns mounted on the mineshaft's walls, with others swinging in their hands. They were a quarter-mile or more into the hillside, chasing veins of silver which, with any luck, would lead back to the mother lode and make the boss man filthy rich, some of it trickling down to Ridpath's pockets, much less for the miners who would find whatever waited there and haul it back to daylight.

As they closed in on the shaft's dead end, Ridpath was conscious of the miners slowing down, then stopping altogether, waiting for him to proceed alone. The Mexicans were off to one side, Chinese on the other, watching him with bright eyes from their mutually dirty faces.

Glaring back at them, the foreman said, "Somebody has to show me what you mean."

A dozen stiff arms pointed toward the darkness just ahead of Ridpath, but the miners moved no closer to the spot where they'd stopped digging before fetching him.

"Goddamn it all to hell!" He snatched one of the lanterns and paced off the last twelve feet or so, then saw where they had broken *through* the wall instead of merely chipping at it with their picks and hammers.

Tools some of them clutched now as if they were weapons meant for self-defense.

"The hell is this? An opening?"

Ridpath held up his lantern, felt its heat against his face as he peered through a crevice ten, twelve inches wide and maybe two feet long from top to bottom. Darkness on the other side absorbed the light and swallowed it, but he could still see—or imagine—something *moving* back in there. He squinted at it, trying for a fix on size and what it might be, when his lamplight was reflected with a gleam from something that seemed wet and *conscious.*

Ridpath felt himself begin to tremble as he muttered, "What the fu—"

The moving, shifting *something* rushed to meet him then. Ponderous weight collided with the wall his men had broken through, and Ridpath could have sworn he saw the cold stone bowing toward him, heard the fissure caused by swinging steel give off a loud crack as it strained and started to expand.

"Jesus!"

Behind him, the Chinese and Mexicans were jabbering, some of them already in flight along the mineshaft, toward the adit and its sunlight. Ridpath stood his ground, holding the lantern high and reaching for the six-gun on his hip to meet whatever might be breaking through the wall, but then the stone sustained another heavy blow and started crumbling outward, fist-sized chunks of rock and larger pieces tumbling at his feet.

He caught a glimpse of *something else* behind the

growing fissure, felt his nerve break to his everlasting shame, and sprinted back along the tunnel in pursuit of the escaping miners. Those who hadn't run already followed him in panic, crying out their heathen oaths of fright.

Ridpath made it to daylight, saw the workers mobbing up outside the adit, still in racially distinct and separate groups. He waved them clear, shouting, "Get back! Move out!" and made a beeline for his humble living quarters as they scattered.

There, some fifty yards out from the shaft's black opening, he left his lantern on the threshold, barged into the shack, and grabbed his Henry rifle from its wall pegs. Cocking it, he turned back toward the Belle Aire Mine and waited while the shadows lengthened for whatever had been breaking through down there to free itself, scrabble along the tunnel, and emerge.

ONE

PRESIDIO COUNTY, TEXAS: JULY 13, 1875

Gideon Thorn woke with a snake coiled on his chest. He didn't move, except to crack one eyelid, taking in the thick curved shape and flat head by the pale light of a waning gibbous moon. It was enough to tell him he was looking at a western diamondback rattler, settled within striking distance of his face.

Thorn was not frightened as another man might be. Surprised, of course, but panic didn't enter into it. He knew that thrashing out from underneath the snake was tantamount to suicide, and Thorn had many things to do before he died.

Instead, remaining still and supine, he reached out to touch the rattler with his mind. It was a skill he had acquired in childhood, or perhaps was born with, letting him communicate to varying degrees with sundry species of the so-called lower orders. As a rule, Thorn did better with mammals than with reptiles or amphibians, had little sway with fish, and none at all with insects or the like. The animals he "touched" did not converse in words, of course, but might respond with images if he was able to connect and they saw fit.

With snakes, on rare occasions when he had reason to contact them, Thorn tried for simple feelings: peace and relaxation were the best, a sense of calm imparted to prevent something unfortunate from happening. This morning, though, he strove for gentle agitation.

When the rattler stirred, Thorn knew that it felt something. He attempted to impart uneasiness, a sense that it was better off elsewhere, beyond the warm body it lay upon and the small campfire dying out nearby. The diamondback stirred slowly, gave a cautionary *tick-tick* with its rattles while it peered into his face and failed to note Thorn's one cracked eyelid.

Finally, around the six- or seven-minute mark, it started to uncoil and spill across the left side of his chest, over his arm and to the ground below, gliding away with no suggestion of unseemly haste, tongue flicking out as if it tasted breakfast on the air, somewhere beyond the human's modest camp.

Thorn rolled to one side, following the reptile with his eyes and reaching out to steer it wide around his animals, the gray stallion he'd named Shadow, standing together with his pack mule, Bell. The diamondback paid them no heed and slithered off toward the horizon, westward, where a razor's edge of dim gray light had slashed the night's blue velvet shot with stars.

Thorn pegged the time as being close to five o'clock, confirmed it with his pocket watch, and rose to start his day. He cracked a can of corned-beef hash and nestled it among the campfire's coals to warm, provided oats to Bell and Shadow from one of the packs the molly mule had carried on her back, and finished dressing in his standard suit of black, including frock coat, vest, and trousers with the cuffs tucked into knee-high boots.

A dagger's grip protruded from the right-hand boot, but it was Thorn's weapon of last resort. His gunbelt supported twin Colt Single Action Army revolvers, the famous "Peacemakers," and a Bowie knife with a twelve-inch blade. When mounted, his firearms included a Winchester Model 1873 lever-action rifle chambered for the same .44-40 rounds as his six-guns, fifteen in its tubular magazine plus one in the chamber, and an 1872 model Sharps rifle in .50-90 caliber, accurate to fifteen hundred yards with its custom-made, three-foot-long scope.

Thorn still had a ride of thirty miles or so to reach New Egypt, where he planned to spend the next few days. He'd been enticed in that direction by a tongue-in-cheek report the *San Antonio Express* had published, playing up a "flying monster" that had crawled out of a silver mine and flapped away, impervious to rifle fire from startled onlookers. Thorn knew the tale might be a hoax, one of the "silly season" fillers certain so-called journalists produced to boost their papers' summer circulation.

On the other hand, if it were true...

According to the article, the massive beast—whatever it might be—had been unearthed by diggers at the Belle Aire Mine, owned by one Randolph Boone, residing in New Egypt. Boone had not been present when the incident occurred, but foreman Seely Ridpath, hailed in print as "a reliable White Man" and a "renowned marksman," had sworn to the account and claimed that he had fired no less than five shots at the creature with a Henry rifle as it lumbered from the mineshaft, spread its wings, and then took to the air, flying away and out of sight into the dusk.

The miners who'd unwittingly discovered it, a crew made up in equal parts of Mexicans and Chinese "celestials," were said to be on strike, refusing to go underground for fear of meeting other monsters in the dark.

Thorn was intrigued but not convinced. He had pursued a number of such stories in the West, some of them baseless rumors, others blatant hoaxes, and a few that tantalized him still, remaining unexplained. This was his first time chasing giant winged creatures, though, and it was worth a detour that would postpone investigation of a cattle-killing "dog-man-thing" reported from the neighborhood of Amarillo.

So many mysteries, so little time.

Thorn used a handkerchief to lift his breakfast can out of the coals and settled down to eat its contents with a spoon. His animals were busy munching oats and he would water them when they were done eating, no driving rush to hit the trail with dawn just breaking in the east.

He had all day. The beast he sought, if it even existed in the flesh, had either fled New Egypt and was lost to him, or it had found someplace to hide. Whatever proved to be the case, he could investigate it for himself and find out if it had the ring of truth. If witnesses could be induced to speak, Thorn could assess them, learn if they had been misrepresented in the article he'd read, and probe for details in their memories.

No problem there, he thought. Someone who'd seen a giant flying monster would remember it, unless he had been driven crazy by the shock.

Thorn's memory of the event that changed his life,

conversely, was a child's and therefore garbled, shrouded in the mists of time. He could recall fragments, the slaughter of his parents and his elder brother, bits and pieces of his own escape from death, but much of it remained a yawning void that he worked constantly to fill.

Some might have said that Thorn's approach was...strange. He'd visited the old homestead, of course, and found the cabin he had conjured out of memory long since demolished, swept away. Two decades lost between the moment of his private tragedy and Thorn's attempt to learn the truth of it had scoured every trace of murder from the land. No old-timers remained to aid him with his quest, so he attacked it from another, more eclectic avenue.

Gideon Thorn collected mysteries, investigated them where that was feasible, and hoped to someday find a pattern hidden in the warp and weft of details gleaned from one account after another. If and when he found that pattern, *maybe* it would lead him to the secret he pursued and craved above all else.

If not...well, what was he supposed to do except keep looking, searching, until he was satisfied or dead?

Thorn's hash was fair, a byproduct of early canning efforts practiced in the Civil War, better for being heated. As he ate, he thought about his best approach to the investigation in New Egypt. Normally he contacted local authorities, whoever they might be, and introduced himself, explaining his arrival and intentions without giving too much of himself away. Thorn had attracted notice from a few small newspapers during his travels through the West, most recently at Tularosa, in New Mexico Territory, but their readership was localized. He was by no means either famous or notorious.

After his first approach, if he was not rebuffed too energetically, Thorn liked to question any witnesses to strange events who would agree to speak with him, then move along to ordinary residents for their opinions, whether they'd seen anything or not. While not a hidebound skeptic, given his own childhood tragedy, Thorn knew from personal experience that fully half or more of all the tales he chased were fabricated or at least exaggerated, some recurring over time in cycles until their immediacy and their source was lost. Still others had some natural solution —animals glimpsed briefly, misidentified; some others natural phenomenon including weather, tricks of light, and odd behavior on the part of well-known frontier denizens.

As for the rest, he still had hope.

Before or after asking questions, Thorn would view the scene of a peculiar incident or sighting, which in this case meant the Belle Aire Mine. He knew that might pose difficulties of its own, since miners were traditionally jealous of their claims and trouble that was publicized meant further headaches for the owners. Randolph Boone, according to the article he'd read, was not a lowly prospector himself, but rather someone who had prospered bringing "color" from the ground in other areas and hoped to make his latest fortune from the Belle Aire with a silver strike that rivaled the Nevada Comstock Lode.

He *had* found silver, but before he started living like a Persian emperor, his men also—allegedly—had loosed a monster on the world.

Whether that proved out true or not, Boone might be the kind of man who would protect his claim until the trouble was resolved, including use of gun thugs if he deemed them necessary. For that reason, if no other, Thorn would have to watch his step around the mine and take no liberties—or none that he was caught at, anyway.

When he was finished eating, Thorn stamped on the can to crush it flat, then buried it, using a spade he had included with his other gear for Bell to carry on their ramblings. His last task, after washing up in the same trickling stream his animals had drunk from overnight, was saddling Shadow and securing Bell's load to the best of his ability, allowing for her comfort. Thorn took time cinching Bell's packsaddle—a complex leather web with ample padding, not the crude wooden devices used by many haulers—and arranging bundles on the framework so that they were balanced, none wearing unduly on her withers, back, or rump. When he was finished, Bell gave him a look and flicker of a thought that it was satisfactory, assuming she was forced to carry goods at all.

Thorn had a map of Texas that included Presidio County, founded in 1850 as a breakaway from San Antonio's more famous Bexar County but formally established in this very year, just months ago. According to his studies, it was rated as the largest county in America, sprawling over twelve thousand square miles. No railroads had arrived yet, but stagecoaches made the rounds and the county seat, Fort Davis, had its own telegraph office now. Elsewhere, Presidio County was desert and mountains, small scattered towns, and mineshafts delving Mother Earth for precious ore.

And possibly, against all odds, a monster winging overhead.

Thorn wasn't seeking silver, but he hoped to know the truth of *that*, at least, before he traveled on.

The miles between his campsite and New Egypt held no great surprise for Thorn. He had expected stark, dry country for the most part, beautiful in its own way, and was not disappointed by the scenery around him as he struck an easy pace for Bell and Shadow. Stopping twice for them to rest and drink at burbling streams, three hours passed before Thorn glimpsed his destination on the skyline, first a small dark smudge, resolving into varied shapes of human structures as he closed the gap.

His watch told him that it was half-past ten o'clock when he approached New Egypt's posted eastern boundary, defining jurisdiction for whatever local law the denizens had set in place. He made a pass through town, down what he took for Main Street though it was not labeled such, and found the livery out toward the settlement's north end, were wafting odors from the animals inside would not disturb the merchants or their customers unduly.

As to smell, there wasn't much, a good sign of a livery whose workers kept it clean. Thorn found the hostler doubling as village blacksmith, hammering a new-made shoe and glad to leave it for a while to wipe his brow and do some business. He was forty-some years old, a trifle on the portly side compared to Thorn, with one cheek swollen by a fat tobacco plug. His rates were reasonable and they both unloaded Bell, stowing Thorn's gear, except the Sharps, inside a room the hostler had constructed and outfitted with a padlock for that very purpose. He assured Thorn that he would be present, or would have a helper at the livery, to open up at any hour of the day or night.

Paid up for two nights in advance, the Sharps balanced across his lap and saddle pommel, Thorn rode back the way he'd come to reach New Egypt's sole hotel,

The Pyramid. Clearly, it had been named to carry on a naming theme, but it bore no resemblance to a real-life pyramid in Old Egypt or in the steaming rainforests of Mexico and South America. It was a plain box of a structure, built from wood already weathered by the desert elements, blue paint fading since the hotel was established, as the sign above its entryway proclaimed, two years ago.

Thorn made a sight—dusty, trail worn, and carrying his two long guns—when he entered the hotel lobby. Even so, the young but balding clerk put on a smile to greet him from behind the registration counter, asking, "May I help you, sir?"

Thorn took a room for two nights with an option to remain, no difficulty for The Pyramid, since he could tell from dangling keys behind the desk that only half its rooms were occupied. Thorn's was located on the second floor, facing the street, the clerk proud to inform him that each floor had its own water closet at the south end of the hallway, each with a flush toilet fully functional. Baths were available "downtown," at Charley Hubbard's barbershop.

Thorn went upstairs, entered his room, and found it more or less what he'd expected for a town New Egypt's size. He had a brass four-poster bed; a dresser with a mirror, chair, washbowl, a pitcher filled with water earlier that morning, and a freestanding chifforobe with hooks inside for hanging clothes, shelves to the left for stacking anything that wouldn't fit the dresser's drawers.

He would retrieve his spare suit and assorted other clothing from the livery when he brought Shadow back, that afternoon. Until then, Thorn slapped trail dust from the outfit he was wearing, wiped his brow, and peered into the mirror at his most distinctive feature, a strip of pure white hair running across his scalp from hairline to the crown, along the track of an old scar.

It marked him, a reminder of the claw that etched that furrow twenty-one years earlier.

But had the owner of that talon meant to kill him, or had he been chosen to survive, wearing the brand, for reasons yet unknown?

Thorn put his flat-brimmed, high-crowned had back on and leaned his Sharps inside the chifforobe. The cabinet possessed no lock, but Thorn removed a loose thread from the quilted comforter and draped it where a hand was certain to disturb it, opening the chifforobe. Leaving, he locked the door behind him, giving it a shake, and then tried out the water closet for his own enlightenment, before he took his Winchester downstairs and out into the street, where Shadow waited for him at a hitching post.

While passing back and forth, he'd scouted out the town's main thoroughfare. Aside from the hotel, the livery and barber's shop, Thorn had picked out the marshal's office; an apparently successful hardware store; a grocery and butcher's shop; a newspaper, *The Hieroglyph*, continuing the town's Egyptian theme; an assay office and a small bank; other offices including those of a physician, two attorneys, and a surveyor; dueling saloons, the Paradise facing the Mother Lode across the town's main avenue, both with their hookers lolling on the upstairs balconies; and a disordered, crowded alley where Thorn saw that all the faces were Chinese.

Feeling a sudden thirst, Thorn stopped outside the Mother Lode, went in, and drank a cold beer standing at the bar. One of the barroom's girls approached him, querying his interest in explicit terms, but Thorn declined with thanks and asked the barkeep for directions to the Belle

Aire Mine. That brought a frown, but he was not denied the information: two miles north-northeast of town, reasonably near another mine, the Silver Crown.

"Steer clear of that one," said the bartender. "They got a raft of itchy-fingered guards around it. Pinkertons."

"But not the Belle Aire?" Thorn inquired.

A lazy shrug. "Since all the workers ran away, I hear it's Seely Ridpath by hisself, foreman for Mr. Boone."

Thorn paid and left a decent tip, then left the bar and mounted Shadow in late morning's glare, the heat already rising past eighty degrees beneath a cloudless sky. Mention of Pinkertons—agents from the "Eye That Never Sleeps," the Chicago-based Pinkerton National Detective Agency—intrigued him. Called "detectives," Thorn knew many of the operatives were no more than guns for hire, notorious for strikebreaking and other measures of harassment against labor unions, also for pursuing road agents such as Missouri's James-and-Younger gang. Their first foray as bodyguards for an exalted person, President Abraham Lincoln, failed when they were absent from Ford's Theater in April 1865.

And could they guard a silver mine against a flying monster?

Thorn let that thought occupy his mind as he rode out of town, watching the skies.

TWO

SILVER CROWN MINE

The bartender had steered him true. Thorn traveled one mile north-northeast of town, then veered off farther to the east, giving himself more room to pass around the Silver Crown Mine without drawing any unwanted attention from the guards. He still wanted a look around the property, however, and he spied a low hill topped with desert willow and burr oak that masked his easterly approach.

When Thorn was in among the trees and looking down upon the Silver Crown, perhaps two thousand yards away, he took a folding spyglass from his saddlebag and opened it, scanning the mine and its surroundings from his cover in the shade. He watched men trundle in and out with wheelbarrows and noted all of them were white, no Mexicans or Chinese such as those who'd fled from the Belle Aire. Their guards were white as well, all dressed in dark suits, though their garments were not matched to qualify as uniforms.

Detectives, Thorn surmised, or what the Pinkerton Detective Agency sent west when guns and muscle were required, in lieu of analyzing clues and solving mysteries. All of the guards wore pistols, and at least half carried lever-action rifles, several others sporting double-barreled shotguns. Thorn counted from left to right and made it twenty men, though he supposed some others may have been in town or down inside the mine.

Most interesting to him was a wagon parked beside the adit of the Silver Crown. A gunman lounged across its high seat, but the eye-catcher stood in its open bed: a Gatling gun mounted atop a tripod, with six barrels and a hand-crank on its right-hand side, a round drum magazine of ammunition rising vertically from its receiver. In expert hands, Thorn knew, the Gatling fired six hundred .58-caliber rounds per minute, although the drum restrained it, holding no more than 240 cartridges. Still, it was a reliable man-shredder at any range under five hundred yards.

But how would it do against giant monsters?

Thorn spent another six or seven minutes studying the mine and its uninterrupted operation, noting how the workers who emerged avoided making eye contact with their protectors. Only when a guard was turned away might one of them glare at his back, perhaps mouth something Thorn assumed was kept under his breath. The miners were not comfortable with the guards—in fact, seemed to despise them—causing Thorn to wonder if the Pinkertons were there for their protection or to keep them on the job despite their fear of what had happened on the Belle Aire claim.

Slave labor was illegal now, since 1865, but if the miners drew a meager check on payday, were the guards considered overseers of a captive labor force? That was a question for the law, beyond Thorn, and he focused on the reason for his ride out from New Egypt as he turned Shadow away.

BELLE AIRE MINE

Another thirty minutes easy riding brought Thorn to the mineshaft where the monster he was hunting had allegedly emerged. He took that with a grain of salt for now, as he did all *outré* reports that he received, waiting to speak with witnesses and judge their stories for himself.

Unlike the Silver Crown, the Belle Aire Mine appeared to be nearly deserted. *Nearly,* because Thorn made out a covered pony trap parked near the open doorway of a little house or shed someone had built within a short jog of the adit. There was no one in the carriage, but whoever drove it out from town had taken time to put a feedbag on the horse before he left it standing harnessed to the vehicle and went inside.

Thorn rode up to the trap and reined in Shadow at the other horse's side with no complaint from the roan gelding with the bag over its nose. When he dismounted and walked casually past the buggy, to its rear, Thorn heard somebody stirring in the clapboard house or shed and saw a shadow fall across the threshold just before a man emerged. He was immediately followed by a second, this one with a pistol belt around his waist, but Thorn could tell the first man through the doorway was the one in charge.

"Help you?" the boss man asked.

"Gideon Thorn."

"I never heard of you."

"I'm guessing you'd be Randolph Boone," Thorn said.

"And you'd be standing on my property if that were true, which is in fact the case. If you're a goddamn Pinkerton—"

"No, sir. I hope to speak with you about your problem here," Thorn told him.

"We don't need no nosy parkers buttin' in," the second man declared, his right hand resting on his pistol's butt.

"I don't mean to disturb you," Thorn replied. "I've read about your trouble in the newspaper."

"Which one?" asked Boone.

"A Texas paper."

"Likely bull-squat, then."

"Only the basics. Panic in the mine, a giant flying monster charging out, surviving rifle fire before it flew away."

"That's what the *miners* claim," Boone said, but with a sidelong glance at his companion which suggested he had seen the creature too—or, at the very least, repeated a description of it.

"Mexicans and Chinese," Thorn observed.

"They love to shirk their labors," Boone said. "And they'd love it more if they could get a union organized—or one for each of their ungodly heathen races—and demand a salary no claim owner could possibly afford."

"So that's your take on it?" Thorn asked. "A ploy to organize?"

"What else?"

"Maybe your foreman there could answer that," Thorn answered.

He was guessing, but the second man had spent the past few minutes staring at his boots, red-faced from something other than the desert sun, and now his eyes came up to lock with Thorn's. "I'm sayin' nothin'," he replied.

"Not even if it's authorized by your employer?"

"Listen now," said Boone. "Before we say another word, I need to know exactly who you are and what your interest is in all of this. Spill it, or climb back on that gray and get the hell away from here."

Thorn knew he'd have to share. The question was, how much?

He made his choice and said, "My name, you know. When I was two years old, in what's now Colorado Territory, something killed my parents and my older brother, leaving me alive. The sheriff blamed a grizzly in the midst of winter, when it should have been asleep, and it was never found. I grew up in the East, came into money, and since then I've been looking for answers in the West."

Boone peered at him with narrowed eyes. "You think this *thing* my miners claim they saw was your wild critter."

"No," Thorn said with perfect confidence. "If it exists, it's something else."

"So why's it interest you?"

Thorn shrugged. "I have no leads to speak of. Anything could be significant somehow."

"Well—"

"Boss," the foreman interrupted him.

They stared at one another for a little while, then Boone said, "Christ. All right. Come in out of the sun and sit a spell while Seely tells you what he *claims* he saw."

Thorn followed them inside the hovel, not as rough as he'd expected from the outside, but still very basic, leaning hard toward crude. The foreman Boone called Seely sat down on a cot, while Thorn and Boone parked on the shack's two chairs.

"I'm Seely Ridpath, foreman here just like you guessed," the nervous man began. He told a sparse, straightforward version of events that had occurred eight days before, from revelation of an unexpected cavern in the Belle Aire Mine, to the explosive exit of a huge and hulking animal that nearly filled the shaft. Emerging from the adit, it had paused as it to sniff the desert air, then had unfolded massive wings and lifted off.

"I shot it five times with my Henry," Ridpath said, pointing to where his rifle hung on wall pegs. "Hit it, too, all five. I never missed nothin' that size at fifty yards. Hellfire, I never *seen* nothin' that big before."

"And there you have it, Mr. Thorn. My diggers—*former* diggers—say the same thing more or less, piling on legends from their homeland to explain it. Me, I've never seen or heard of anything like it. I don't doubt Seely's word, or what he *thinks* he saw, and I would swear he damn well wasn't drinking on the job."

"I wadn't," Ridpath said, raising a hand as if he were about to take an oath in court.

"I hope to speak with some of your miners," Thorn said.

"*Ex*-miners. Any man walks off a job of mine unless he's hurt or deathly ill, I fire his ass."

"Who digs the silver, then?" asked Thorn.

"No one, apparently."

Thorn nodded. "But if someone could unravel this, locate the beast and deal with it..."

"Someone like you?" Boone asked.

"With any help available," Thorn said.

"Well, that would prove the miners right—and Seely, too, of course. I'd have to take 'em back if they were willing to return."

"About this cavern in the mine," Thorn said. "Has anyone explored it?"

"We went in the day after the scare," Boone said, nodding toward Ridpath. "With the marshal from New Egypt and a couple of his deputies. There wasn't any monster big or little, but..." He caught himself and heaved a sigh.

"But what?" asked Thorn.

"I don't know you from Adam," Boone replied, "but I will have your word of honor that you keep this next bit to yourself."

"You have it," Thorn agreed.

"Inside that cavern there are veins of silver eight feet wide and more. We found the goddamned mother lode, and then some."

"With no miners to extract it."

"How d'you like that pisser?"

"Sitting on a fortune," Thorn observed. "It's in your own best interest to be done with this as soon as possible."

Boone's eyes narrowed again. "Uh-huh. And what's that gonna cost me? What's the going rate for monster hunts these days?"

"I won't be charging you, and I can't promise you results," Thorn said. "I'll find out what I can and do my best. We'll let it go at that."

"And if you can't do anything?"

"Then you're no worse off than before."

"Well, shit. I never thought I'd be this old and find my life's dream stymied by some monster from a fairy tale."

"If it's alive, it's not a fairy tale," said Thorn. "Before I go, I'm wondering about the Silver Crown."

"That bastard Hearst," Boone said, almost spitting the name.

"Is he a local prospector?"

"George Hearst? Not hardly," Boone replied. "Believe I heard he comes from somewhere in Missouri, but he's based in California since the gold rush back in '49. Made money around Sutter's Mill, and at Grass Valley, then he struck it rich mining Nevada's Comstock Load. Spreads tales that he hears whispers from the earth and lives to dig the 'color' out. A lot of superstitious claptrap, but he's in tight with the politicians and the Pinkertons."

"Speaking of which, I passed the Silver Crown while I was riding out here," Thorn remarked. "Your Mr. Hearst has guards crawling all over, plus a Gatling gun."

"I told you. And he's not *my* Mr. Hearst. Believe me when I say that he'd do *anything* to fasten on a claim like mine, and when the word gets out about our latest find he'll go to work with everything he's got."

"Which is?" Thorn asked.

"His private army, if it comes to that. Before he starts in killing, though, he'll likely try to have my claim invalidated by the men he owns at Fort Davis. Failing that, he'll likely try the state authorities in Austin, spread some cash around and tell 'em I can't work the claim because my miners all ran off. I wouldn't be surprised to find myself evicted in another month or two, but if he can't swing that, it comes back down to war."

"With you outnumbered and outgunned," Thorn said.

"Same thing they said at Gettysburg in '63," Boone answered. "But we held the ridge and put them down."

Thorn changed the subject. "Riding past and looking in, it seemed that most of Hearst's miners are white," he said.

"They's *all* white," Ridpath said. "Them Cornishmen."

"He loves to use the Cornish," Boone elaborated. "Ever since the mining in their homeland went to hell, thousands have immigrated to America, looking for jobs they recognize. The big advantage is they all speak English and they know the business coming in, so Hearst isn't required to teach 'em like celestials and Mexicans. The *trouble* is they work for pennies to begin with, then they start to grumble about forming unions. The Chinese and Mexicans don't think that way."

"So he's been having trouble?" Thorn inquired.

"It's relative," said Boone. "Too many of them try to organize, his Pinkertons kill off the leaders and the others settle down. I wouldn't be surprised if George's guards around the Silver Crown are there to keep the miners in, as much as keeping anybody out."

Thorn took a leap and said, "You think that Hearst's behind your monster problem, Mr. Boone?"

That brought a frown. "If it was only stories spread among the heathens, I'd say yes without a heartbeat's hesitation, Mr. Thorn. But even George Hearst, talking to the earth and all, can't dream a real-life monster out of nothing at the bottom of a mine."

"No, sir," Thorn said. "I guess he can't." Turning to Ridpath, he inquired, "You're absolutely sure of what you saw?"

The foreman's eyes were haunted as he answered, "Sure as anything I ever seen."

Thorn nodded. Said, "If you have no objection, Mr. Boone, I need to meet your miners."

"Sure, why not? César Estrada does the talking for the Mexicans. A Chinaman called Wu Chengjun leads the celestials. He's tied in with the tongs from overseas, one of their secret brotherhoods. Runs opium and whores along with laundries for the white folk and his labor contracting."

Rising, Thorn said, "I'll see what I can learn and let you know."

Thorn pointed Shadow back toward town, sent him a mental image of New Egypt, and allowed the horse to find his own way. Thorn, soon lost in thought, glanced toward the sky sporadically but saw no evidence of huge winged creatures circling overhead. He *did* see vultures halfway though his journey, wheeling in the air above some carcass they had found, and steered Shadow to find it on the off chance that it was a fallen monster, finished off at last by Seely Ridpath's rifle shots the week before.

Alas, it was a common pronghorn antelope, its cause of death unclear, swollen and ripe for picking in the Texas desert sun. Thorn left the buzzards to it, turned his stallion back toward town, and let his mind go wandering.

He didn't buy the thought of George Hearst cooking up a monster just to put his rival out of business. Nor did Randolph Boone, despite his early pose of blaming the events on frightened, superstitious immigrants. As for the foreman, Seely Ridpath, he'd seen *something,* but he couldn't put a name to it.

Neither could Thorn.

At Harvard University, before he had abandoned studying the law, zoology had been among the courses in his bachelor's curriculum. Thorn knew the largest birds of North America—at least, the species known to science—were the California condor; the two eagle species, bald and golden; and the turkey vulture, ranked in order of their wingspans. In his travels, Thorn had also picked up rumors of a giant "thunderbird," known to the native tribes for centuries and glimpsed, some said, by white men since they'd pushed beyond the Appalachians, headed west.

Leaving the thunderbirds aside, perhaps extinct by now or purely mythical, Thorn knew the wingspan of his home-land's largest birds ranged from nearly ten feet in the condor down to six feet for the largest vulture. There were other condors, in the Andes range of South America, whose wingspan might be twelve feet wide, but none of them could match the creature Seely Ridpath and his workmen had reported seeing at the Belle Aire Mine.

And no known species of large birds in the Americas lived underground.

That was the other puzzler in this mystery, as troubling as the beast's identity. Boone's miners had discovered their rich cavern, now abandoned, far below ground, sealed off from the world of sun and air and food above. Thorn knew —thanks to zoology again—that many small creatures thrived underground, feeding on one another or the plants they found there, some of them bleached white and blind from countless generations in the dark. The Belle Aire crea-ture, though, was obviously something else. It rushed to flee the mine when liberated, but how long had it been trapped below? How long could any large beast live in those conditions, waiting for an opportunity to take the air?

As he approached New Egypt and its livery, Thorn knew no more of any substance than when he had started out that morning. He believed that Seely Ridpath and the miners had seen something. As to what it was and where it might have gone, he'd ponder that over his dinner at The Pyramid and as he tried to sleep.

THREE

NEW EGYPT, TEXAS

Thorn saw Shadow rightly settled at the livery, checked in on Bell, then took his Winchester and saddlebags back to The Pyramid. His room was undisturbed as far as he could tell, no reason why it should have been invaded in his absence, though that sometimes changed in small towns when the rumors of his local mission got around.

Thorn's stomach growled, but dinner service in the hotel's restaurant didn't begin till six o'clock, leaving the better part of three hours for him to kill before he ate. First thing, he stripped, brushed down the suit he wore for traveling, and hung it with its matching mate, inside the chifforobe. He'd wear the clean one down to dinner, then switch off again tomorrow, when he made the rounds in hope of landing more eyewitness evidence.

Or lies and fables, as the case might be.

Thorn shaved next, finishing the water in the pitcher that the hotel had provided. That was not a problem, since he'd seen the fancy water closet at the far end of his hallway and confirmed that its equipment featured both the famous flushing toilet and a sink. Before he went to sleep that night, he'd fill the pitcher with fresh water for the morning, no need to alert the hotel's staff for such a trivial pursuit.

When he had rid himself of stubble, Thorn stretched out on the four-poster bed, his gunbelt coiled beside him, not unlike the diamondback who'd started out that morning on his chest. Both packed a deadly punch for the unwary—or, where Thorn's Colts were concerned, *twelve* punches before he had to reload.

Not that he expected trouble, but it seemed to follow him.

Thorn planned to nap, but couldn't get the hang of it at first. His mind was busy turning over what he'd heard from Randolph Boone and Seely Ridpath, thinking of the guards around the nearby Silver Crown, wondering if the man who ran that operation was the ogre Boone described him as, or just a standard robber baron like the others who made news from coast to coast.

The very rich—including Thorn's own forebears and his Aunt Drusilla, who had saved him from a Kansas Territory orphanage when he was two years old—were *different*. Thorn seldom felt that way himself, since he'd inherited the bulk of Aunt Drusilla's fortune two years earlier, but it was true he could pull certain strings if necessary, call on various important men for aid in an emergency. He shied away from it on principle, preferring not to be in anybody's debt, but he knew well enough the varied ways in which Big Money moved and shook society.

Considering George Hearst, he thought of others in the same league, some of whom he'd met in passing, others who were legends in their own time, rising to the pinnacle of industry and commerce, sitting comfortably atop fortunes beyond calculation. Thorn had never met John Jacob Astor, but he knew some of the great man's heirs. He'd dined with Andrew Carnegie on one occasion, courtesy of Aunt Drusilla, and had glimpsed railroading's E. H. Harriman across a crowded room. Others on the same level —Jay Cooke, J. P. Morgan, Cornelius Vanderbilt, Jay Gould, Henry Frick and John D. Rockefeller—were acquainted with Thorn's aunt and may have heard his name, but they were not his kind.

The city rich had other passions, chiefly the pursuit of money, even though they had enough to live a thousand lifetimes in the fashion of medieval potentates. Thorn's quest lay elsewhere, running down the truth of what had happened to his family, piercing the veil of other possibly related mysteries along the way. He'd never occupy a boardroom or direct the fate of workers in their tens of thousands, but it suited Thorn.

And while that thought soothed him a bit, he drifted off to sleep.

Thorn woke at half-past five o'clock precisely, thankful for the mental discipline that curbed a tendency to oversleep. He dressed in black as usual and left his hat behind when he locked up his room. The streak of white along his old scalp scar was a reminder of his private tragedy, but it did not embarrass Thorn. Most people caught themselves if they began to gape at it and turned their eyes away. For those who asked about it, Thorn supplied answers dictated by his mood.

The hotel's dining room was large enough to seat

multiple occupants from all its rooms at once, though half of them were empty at the present time. Two couples had arrived ahead of Thorn, heads bent and poring over menus as he entered. A young waitress welcomed him and led Thorn to a small table for two, positioned near a window facing on the street, and granting Thorn a narrow view into the hotel's lobby.

When he saw the menu, Thorn decided that he wasn't simply hungry; he was ravenous. He ordered up a T-bone steak, medium rare, with baked potato, green peas, and creamed cauliflower on the side, reserving judgment on desert until he saw how all of that went down. The waitress brought him coffee first, piping and black, while Thorn surveyed the street outside and left his fellow diners to themselves. The window's glass reflected *them* observing *him*, and that was fine. He didn't mind attention, to a point, but liked it to be unobtrusive, most particularly when he dined alone.

Only a moment seemed to pass before the waitress laid his plate in front of him. It looked and smelled delicious, an impression instantly confirmed as Thorn dug in with knife and fork. He savored every bite—until the nearly mirrored glass beside him showed a man approaching from the kitchen, striding confidently toward his table.

Thorn ignored the stranger standing over him until the new arrival asked, "How do you find your supper, sir?"

"The waitress brought it to me," Thorn replied, raising his eyes to meet those of a man who wore a checkered vest under his gray wool suit. The stranger had a spade-shaped beard shot through with gray, more salt-and-pepper showing in his relatively short hair, parted on the right.

"I am referring to its quality," the stranger said.

"I can't complain."

"My Aunt Lou is the chef," his visitor proclaimed.

"And who are you?" Thorn asked.

"George Hearst. I own The Pyramid."

"And your aunt's working in the kitchen?"

"Well, I call her that. Aunt Lou's my nigger cook."

"I see. Give her my compliments, will you?"

"I'd rather have a conversation with you, Mr. Thorn," Hearst said.

"Just now?" Thorn didn't try to mask his frown.

"There's no time like the present, eh?"

Hearst sat across from Thorn without an invitation, smiling thinly through his beard, hands folded on the tabletop as if he were preparing to say grace.

"Why would a busy man like you take time to learn my name?" Thorn asked.

"I like to know all of the guests in my hotel, which, at the moment, can be counted on the fingers of my hands with digits still remaining."

"I'm referring to your interests in mining."

"Ah. Well, yes, there's that. Finding the color takes priority with me, but I enjoy a certain measure of diversity. And you?"

"Just passing through," Thorn said.

"Unless you find a monster?"

Thorn suppressed the urge to cock an eyebrow. "How would you know that?" he asked.

"I've found through hard experience that ignorance is far from bliss. Do you put any stock in these reports?"

"I couldn't say. So far, I've only spoken to a couple of the witnesses."

"One witness and his boss," Hearst said, correcting him. "You'll want to quiz the Mexicans and Chinks next, I surmise?"

Instead of answering, Thorn asked a question of his own. "Do you routinely denigrate the other races, Mr. Hearst?"

The mining magnate blinked at that. "What do you mean, sir?"

"The Chinese are 'Chinks' to you. Your Aunt Lou is a 'nigger'."

"I am known as a plain-spoken man," Hearst said.

"Sometimes a euphemism for the plainly crude."

A tinge of color stained Hearst's cheeks above his beard. "I wish to know your interest in this so-called monster, sir."

"My interest," Thorn advised him, "is my own. If you'll excuse me now..."

"Of course," Hearst answered stiffly, rising from his chair. "Accept a brief word of advice from one who knows. Be careful, Mr. Thorn. These mining camps are dangerous."

"Thank you for your concern," Thorn told the portly man's retreating back.

"Young upstart. Interloper! Damn his eyes!"

Hearst paced his suite, if you could rightly call it that, on the third floor of his hotel. His solitary guest—Clete Alford, leader of the Pinkerton detachment covering the Silver Crown on orders from Chicago—watched the mining baron work himself into a rage.

"Who does he think he is, putting me off that way, within my own goddamned hotel?"

That was a question. Alford answered, "I don't know, sir."

Turning on him, Hearst replied, "And that's the problem, Clete. That is the problem in a nutshell."

"Sir?"

"I need further information on this youngster," Hearst replied. "Reach out to Pinkerton headquarters. Find out anything you can about it, quickly. Time is of the essence, Clete. You know what that means?"

"Yes, sir. That'll mean a ride up to Fort Davis for the nearest telegraph connection. It's an overnight at best, more if they have to dig around for what you need."

"Sooner your rider leaves the better, then," said Hearst.

"Yes, sir. It would be helpful if I gave HQ a starting place to run the search from."

"There's a hint of Boston in his voice," Hearst said. "He's done his best to master it but hasn't gotten rid of it entirely. A little of the broad 'A' when he isn't careful, with a trace of non-rhoticity."

"Sir?"

"Never mind. Try Boston first and go from there if necessary, on the East Coast."

"Yes, sir!"

Alford let himself out of the suite and Hearst continued pacing, restless. He had spies in place around New Egypt, naturally, as he did in every mining town or camp he colonized. The Mother Lode's bartender had relayed the basics on a stranger asking for directions to the Belle Aire Mine, and his description matched The Pyramid's new lodger, which had given Hearst a name. He had arranged to meet the stranger, confident that he could either charm him or intimidate him, but it hadn't quite worked out that way.

Which was unusual. Infuriating.

He would know the truth about Gideon Thorn, but in the meantime Hearst was left to speculate. Thorn was a young man, early twenties, but he had an air of confidence about him, as if he'd been forced to prove himself repeatedly. The guns he wore, a certain flintiness around Thorn's eyes, suggested that it had been physically, perhaps a struggle to the death.

Or more than one?

Hearst knew his share of killers, hired them when he had to, and they carried out his bidding on command. This one was different, an independent sort, and *driven*. As to what was driving him, that still remained to be revealed.

Could he be working for a rival? Possibly for Randolph Boone?

If that were true, it changed things in New Egypt, but not radically. No matter what his skill and past experience, Thorn couldn't stand against Hearst's small army of Pinkertons, with more on tap if it were necessary. He would die like any other man who tried to thwart his betters and was trampled for his pains.

But if he didn't work for Boone, then what in hell was *really* going on?

Thorn finished off his meal after the interruption by his host and owner of The Pyramid, together with the Silver Crown and who knew what all else around New Egypt. Their encounter did not cow him. On the contrary, when he had cleaned his plate he felt a sudden craving for desert, ordering apple pie with cheese from Hearst's "Aunt Lou."

And while he savored that, he ticked off what he knew about George Hearst. The mining mogul was a rich man, obviously, and a racial bigot, which was nothing extraordinary in the so-called Land of Opportunity, for wealthy white men or their underlings. The fact that he pretended not to recognize his prejudice was passing odd, but Thorn had met others among the upper crust of Boston and New York who took inferiority for granted when it came to other races, other cultures.

More importantly, Hearst was a man who got things done. His wealth proved that, in part, though some men were so rich in what reporters sometimes called the Gilded Age, they simply wallowed in their luxury, letting investments multiply their money while they idled time away in vain pursuits of folly. Hearst did not fit that mold, roaming through the West in search of "color" that would swell his bank accounts, placing himself at risk in rowdy mining camps and making them his own, like an invading general on the march. Based on his reputation, people who opposed him soon were driven out of business, or they died. The cause of death might be a seeming accident, a suicide, or unsolved murder, all of which accomplished the same end.

If Hearst regarded Thorn as any kind of threat, the danger that resulted would be real, immediate. With that in mind, when he went back upstairs, Thorn double-checked his room for any trace of searching in his absence and, again, found none.

For peace of mind, he wedged the room's sole straight-backed chair under the inside doorknob after locking it, an extra measure of security. He also drew the blinds, but left the lantern burning as he stretched out on the bed and turned his thought toward what he hoped he might accomplish in the morning.

Boone had given him two names, spokesmen for workers who had quit the Belle Aire Mine after their "monster" fright. Thorn would attempt to contact both of them tomorrow, but if they refused speak with him, he'd need another angle of attack. Combing the desert and surrounding mountains individually, hunting for some giant unknown creature, struck him as a waste of time. If it was seen so easily, the miners or New Egypt's townsfolk would have tracked it down by now—unless the bulk of local whites dismissed it as a fantasy.

Thorn's mind looped back to Hearst. Assuming that he wanted Boone to fail, and thereby seize his claim, how could he orchestrate the Great Unknown's abrupt appearance at the bottom of the Belle Aire Mine? It seemed impossible, but with a fortune at Hearst's fingertips, was *anything* beyond his grasp?

A racket in the street below disturbed Thorn's train of thought. He rose, crossed to the room's window, and opened it. As he looked out upon the thoroughfare, he saw men rushing past him to the south, where loud and angry voices swelled beyond his line of sight. From his initial tour of New Egypt, Thorn surmised the noise was coming from what whites referred to as Celestial Alley.

Was it mayhem in the making?

Strapping on his gunbelt, pulling on his boots, Thorn donned his coat and hat, removed the chair that jammed his door, and locked the door behind him as he made his way downstairs.

FOUR

Seth Rockwell, marshal of New Egypt, missed the first screams from Celestial Alley, but he heard the rising din that followed from his office on the thoroughfare. He left, locking the door securely, and jogged south a block to reach the cramped and filthy quarters of the town's Chinese inhabitants, where men's and women's voice wailed and jabbered as if terrified and angry all at once.

Rockwell had no idea how many Chinese packed themselves into the narrow side street, unpaved like the town's main thoroughfare but so congested that three men walking abreast felt like a crowd. The street began with laundries, steaming through the daylight hours, and stretched on from there past hovels stacked atop each other, gambling dens, at least two brothels, and a slaughterhouse of sorts at the far end, with squealing pigs penned up outside. Rockwell knew for a fact that there were places on the street where opium was sold and smoked, but he left them alone, since they were not illegal and some white townsfolk were patrons of the vice.

Fights were occasional along Celestial Alley, but the

sounds that Rockwell followed on his trek tonight weren't riotous. Not yet, at least. If forced to say, he would have called them mournful, with a hefty dash of fear thrown in for leavening.

Around him, as he neared the site of tumult, whites were streaming toward the alley, anxious for a glimpse of whatever had stirred the Chinese into high-pitched ruction. On arrival at the alley's mouth, lighted in part by lanterns hanging overhead along its length, the first face that Seth recognized was that of Angelina Farnum, editor and publisher of the camp's newspaper, *The Heiroglyph*. Aside from being helplessly in lust for her—he'd asked her out to dinner half a dozen times, always rebuffed with utmost courtesy—Rockwell was pricked by worry at her presence in the company of so many aroused Chinese.

Approaching her, he asked, "What are you doing here?" without a preamble or salutation.

"Same thing you are, I expect," she answered tartly. "Trying to discover what the matter is."

"That's lawman's work," Rockwell replied.

"And a reporter's to *report*," she said. Glancing around at white folks starting to surround them, Angelina added, "What about these others? Will you ask them all the same question?"

Seth felt himself begin to blush, thankful that it was nearly dark despite the swaying lanterns and the flicker of a nearby streetlight, one of forty torches that illuminated portions of the thoroughfare from dusk till dawn.

"I don't...they..." Rockwell gave it up and closed his mouth, completely at a loss for words.

"That's what I thought," said Angelina, with a wicked smile.

A Chinese taller than most of his countrymen pushed

through the yellow throng inside the alley, scanned white faces on its fringe, and spotted Rockwell's badge. He stepped in front of Rockwell, careful not to glance at Angelina as he said, "You round-eye law."

"That's right," Seth said. "What's happening?"

"You come, you see. Terrible thing!"

"What about me?" asked Angelina, forcing the Chinese to look at her. She let him see a notebook and a pencil as if they were bona fides of her journalistic trade. "I'm from *The Heiroglyph*."

Seth frowned, began to say, "He doesn't know—"

"Newspaper good!" the Chinese cut him off. "Come too!"

"Perfect," said Angelina, with another smirking grin at Rockwell. "I come too."

Ignoring questions from a couple of the other whites standing around, Rockwell followed the tall celestial into the teeming alley, nostrils flaring at the smells of their exotic food, offal around the slaughterhouse, and something he suspected might be burning opium. Seth glanced behind, ensuring Angelina had not separated from him, then pressed on to keep up with their guide.

They reached the far end of the alley, nothing much beyond it but a landfill and the endless desert. Rockwell trailed their escort to the pigpen where a clutch of large and filthy porkers snorted consternation over the disturbance to their evening. Outside the pen, he saw a group of five or six Chinese standing apart from the excited throng. The only man Seth recognized among them was the alley's unofficial mayor and spokesman, Wu Chengjun.

Wu left the others, intercepted Rockwell, and announced, "You law," as if Seth might not know he wore a badge.

"What's all the ruckus here?" Rockwell replied, without acknowledging the obvious.

"An *èxing lóng* attacks one of our people. Carries him away."

"An ex-what?" Rockwell queried, well aware of Angelina scribbling away beside him.

"In your tongue is flying dragon," Wu replied. If he was joking, Rockwell couldn't tell it from his dour and ageless face.

"A flying dragon." Seth tried to remain deadpan, rather than laugh aloud at Wu. "How long ago was this?"

"Five minute, mebbe ten."

"And where'd it happen?"

"There." Wu turned and pointed toward a dark spot on the ground beside the pigpen, leading Seth and Angelina to it.

Rockwell crouched and eyed a large, dark stain on soil, avoided touching it, but sniffed the copper scent of fresh blood in the air. Of course, that might have been the slaughterhouse, one door past where the hogs waited their turn. Now closer, though, Seth saw a trail of similar but smaller stains leading away, out toward the landfill from the largest saturation point. He rose and followed them, surprised when they abruptly terminated.

"Stops here," he told Angelina, for her notebook.

"Dragon fly away with Chan Li Gong."

"The missing man," Seth said. He looked around, shrugged helplessly, and said, "You're sure he's not around here somewhere?"

"Gone!" Wu stubbornly replied. "You find!"

"I find? Which way did this thing carry him off to?" Seth asked.

Wu pointed vaguely toward the desert, mostly darkened now. "That way."

"Well, now, you understand all that out there's beyond my jurisdiction, yes?" Seth caught himself beginning to speak louder, force of habit, tossing in his rough attempt to translate certain terms. "I can't go there. Marshal no lookee."

At his elbow, Angelina muttered to herself, "For heaven's sake!"

"You go," Wu said. "Look there!"

"Illegal," Rockwell said, raising a hand to tap his badge. "Town only."

"Seth," the lady said, "you ride over that desert all the time."

"For *hunting*, Angelina, or to give my horse some exercise. Not law work. That's the county sheriff's territory." Turning back to Wu, he said, "If Chan doesn't come home within a day or two, I'll send a message to the sheriff at Fort Davis. *He* in charge of *that*." Waving his arm to indicate the sweep of arid landscape.

Wu just stared at him, then made a grunting sound and turned away. "There goes my interview," said Angelina. "Thanks for nothing, Seth."

"He barely speaks the language anyway. Listen, why don't we—"

"Not a chance," she said, and turned back toward the thoroughfare.

Gideon Thorn walked two blocks south from The Pyramid to Celestial Alley, arriving as a lawman and a reasonably pretty woman with a notebook in her hand emerged. They were not speaking to each other now, but Thorn got the impression that they'd argued recently and neither was inclined to grant the other's point.

Thorn planned to meet New Egypt's marshal later, possibly tomorrow, but he sensed tonight was wrong and was about to sidestep the unhappy couple when the lawman called to him, "Hey, you!"

Thorn stood and waited for the marshal and his auburn-haired companion to approach.

"Are you one a them Pinkertons?" the marshal asked.

"I am not," Thorn replied. "But it's the second time today somebody's asked me that."

"You have the look."

"Do I?" Thorn glanced down at his suit and shrugged. "Alas."

"Who are you, then?" the local law demanded.

"Thorn. Gideon Thorn. A guest at the hotel, spending a few days here in town."

"Because...?"

"It's here?" Thorn answered with a question of his own.

"Now listen, you—"

"What are you doing, Seth?" the woman cut him off. "Trying to scare off visitors to New Egypt?"

Thorn wasn't scared, but now the woman with the notebook had intrigued him. "Thank you, ma'am," he said.

Her smile flicked on and off like one of those new incandescent light bulbs patented three year ago by Russian Alexander Lodygin, but she did not respond. Thorn turned back to the marshal, who was looking frustrated, weighing his words before he spoke again.

At last he said, "Well, may I ask what brings you to New Egypt?"

"Certainly you may," Thorn said.

When he did not elaborate, the lawman sighed and said, "What *is* it, then?"

"Your monster at the Belle Aire Mine. I'm looking into it."

"As what?" the marshal asked.

Before Thorn could reply, the woman said, "He means in what capacity."

"I took the marshal's meaning, ma'am." Then, to his interrogator, he said, "I take an interest in such things. Call it my avocation if you like."

"You take an interest in *monsters*." Skepticism freighted down the lawman's tone.

"In any strange or unexplained phenomena," Thorn said. "But monsters in particular."

"And why, pray tell?" the marshal, still anonymous, inquired.

"That would be personal," Thorn said.

"Uh-huh. Well, *this*," he pointed toward Celestial Alley, "seems to be a crime scene. These Chinese fight all the time, kill one another now and then, they come and go..."

"Seth!" the woman chided him. "You heard Wu say that it was—"

"Angelina, please be quiet!" snapped the marshal. "We don't know this man from Adam, and I don't believe in—"

"Flying dragons?" she supplied.

"That's right. I don't believe in fairy stories."

"But you saw—"

"Enough! You wanna stand around all night, looking at stains on dirt, go on and be my guest." Turning to Thorn, he said, "And you, I'd caution against snooping around here. White folks don't understand celestials, their lingo and their ways, what sets 'em off."

"Seth Rockwell!" From what Thorn could see, he'd left the woman flustered and upset.

"That's all I'm gonna say about it," Rockwell called over his shoulder as he started north along the thoroughfare.

"Well, I'll be damned," the woman said. She faced toward Thorn, saying, "Excuse my language, Mr. Thorn."

"I've heard worse," he admitted.

"Now, about your interest in monsters..."

"Who are you, again?"

"Oh, please forgive me. Angelina Farnum, editor and publisher of the New Egypt *Heiroglyph*."

"That's quit a title."

"Well, we have a sort of theme in town."

"I noticed, from The Pyramid."

"It stops there, more or less," she said.

"Best not to stretch it out too thin."

"Now, back to—"

"What did the Chinese tell you about a flying dragon?"

Angelina peered at him, deciding whether she should answer, then said, "Only that it flew in here and grabbed one of their people, Chan Li Gong." The name came from her notebook, Angelina glancing quickly at the open page.

"And you believe it?" Thorn inquired.

"Well, there's a stain down at the far end of the alley. Could be blood. It leads off toward the desert, then just...stops."

"Suggesting that a victim had been lifted off the ground."

"I don't know what to think," she said. "And *I'm* supposed to be the one questioning *you*."

"Another time, perhaps," he said. "It's getting late."

"It's barely nine o'clock," she said.

"And I've come off a long ride from the east, plus seeing what there is to see around New Egypt."

"People think we're going places," Angelina said.

Thorn thought of vanished Chan Li Gong and said, "I wouldn't be surprised."

"You *will* sit for an interview tomorrow?" Angelina pressed him.

"I still have a lot to do," he said, "but I sit down for meals at the hotel."

"Is that an invitation?"

Was she turning coy? Thorn said, "I sit, I eat, and I can usually talk at the same time, despite the manners I was raised with."

"If I asked *when* you sit down to eat..."

"Things being equal, I believe the dinner hour would be best."

"The Pyramid starts dishing up at six o'clock."

"They did today."

"Perhaps I'll see you then," she said.

Thorn smiled, thinking, *Perhaps you will.*

As Angelina moved crossed the thoroughfare and moved along its eastern sidewalk, Thorn turned back for one last look at the hubbub in Celestial Alley. It was too much to push in and try to glimpse the bloodstains Angelina had described, an insult to the grief of those who lived along that narrow, crowded street, and frankly dangerous.

Another time, he thought, and turned back northward—to discover that an elderly Chinese man blocked his way. The man, no more than five feet tall, peered up at him and said, "You hunt dragon."

It hadn't been a question, but Thorn felt obliged to answer anyway. He nodded. Said, "I do."

"You come here nine o'clock tomorrow morning, said the Chinaman. "Ask to see Wu Chengjun."

That name again. "Ask whom?" Thorn queried.

"Anyone. All know Wu in Celestial Alley."

The nickname sounded strange, coming from Chinese lips. Thorn understood there was confusion as to its first use. Some whites apparently believed that Chinese people came from outer space, some distant planet. Those with better sense allegedly applied the name because some Chinese called their homeland the "Celestial Empire," a traditional name with its roots lost in ancient history. Either way, coming from this old man, it had the feeling of a self-imposed insult.

"Just anyone at all," Thorn said, confirming it.

The man nodded, said, "Nine o'clock" again, and left Thorn standing there alone.

"Good-night to you, too," he told no one, turning back toward his hotel. He saw no sign of Marshal Rockwell on the short walk back, but lamps were burning in the lawman's office. Thorn passed by and left him to whatever work he might be doing, confident that no approach to Rockwell in his present mood would yield helpful results.

Authorities in towns he'd traveled through regarded Thorn with varying degrees of curiosity, suspicion, and hostility. Lawmen traditionally didn't like the citizens they called "civilians" asking questions of them, watching them, or otherwise "meddling" in their official business. Some were wise enough to know they needed help in certain situations, took it as it came, and were appropriately grateful if it all worked out. Others would rather leave a crime unsolved than have it figured out by someone else, much less a stranger and outsider.

Thorn knew he would have to walk on eggshells around Marshal Rockwell. As for Angelina Farnum, though...

Newspaper people, as he'd lately seen in Tularosa, often had their fingers on the pulse of local happenings, and unlike lawmen with their secrets, journalists were pledged to share the truth with anyone and everyone. Add onto that the fact that Angelina was attractive, and Thorn thought it might be pleasant working with her—to a point, at least. If there was danger in New Egypt, and he'd judge that soon enough, Thorn would not place her life at risk along with his.

But, on the other hand, could he restrain her if she had a true reporter's nose for news?

First find out what the news is, Thorn decided, as he entered his hotel. There was no sign of George Hearst and the dining room was empty at that hour, its tables already set up for breakfast service. Thorn climbed to the second floor and made his first stop at the water closet, where he washed his face and hands, used the flush toilet, and then washed his hands a second time.

The benefits of sanitation in a modern age.

Thorn let himself into his room and lit a lantern, then went back to close and lock the door, wedging the chair beneath its knob again. The thread he'd placed over the handle of the chifforobe hung undisturbed. Drawing the curtains shut against observers from the thoroughfare, he first disarmed, then stripped again and hung his suit up with its mate inside the cabinet.

The whole time, he was pondering the incident from Celestial Alley, wondering why he had been invited—or was it commanded?—to meet Wu Chengjun tomorrow. It had been an item on his mental list, along with questioning César Estrada, but Thorn wondered how the rumored tong leader had known he was in town, much less that he was interested in the "dragon" story.

It was possible, Thorn guessed, that someone might have seen him near the alley, huddled with the marshal and the editor, and even overheard their dialogue. But why would Wu have summoned *him,* a stranger whom it seemed impossible for Wu to know, even by name or reputation from afar?

Ask him tomorrow, Thorn decided. *Ask him anything that comes to mind.*

And so he would, unless their meeting proved to be some kind of trick, even a trap. But once again, Thorn had to pose the question *why?* Wu and his fellow Chinese in New Egypt had no motive in the world for harming Thorn. Nor did it seem they wished to cover up details about the "monster," since they'd told their story to the marshal and *The Heiroglyph*'s reporter, editor, whatever.

No, Thorn decided, he should be all right tomorrow when he went to visit Wu Chengjun.

But he would take along his six-guns, just in case.

FIVE

NEW EGYPT: JULY 14, 1875

Thorn shaved, dressed for the day, and came downstairs just as the hotel's restaurant was opening for breakfast service. From a menu chalked on slate, he ordered scrambled eggs and bacon, fried potatoes topped with sausage gravy, and a mug of coffee he'd been craving since he woke at five o'clock, from a confused and now forgotten dream. He wore his hat, which seemed to be the style for breakfast in New Egypt, while the restaurant filled up around him and the shopkeepers began preparing for another day along the thoroughfare.

The food was tasty, hot, and plentiful, all Gideon expected from a meal when he was traveling. He took his time with it, nearly three hours still remaining until Wu Chengjun expected him. Meanwhile, he watched for George Hearst but saw nothing of the mining baron stirring in his own establishment.

And what about "Aunt Lou"? Would she be slaving in the hotel's kitchen over breakfast, lunch, and dinner? Thorn tried dredging up the proper outrage, but decided that he didn't care, as long as he was served the best available in town each time he sat down in the restaurant.

When he was done, his bill paid, Thorn went out to look around New Egypt in the morning's light. In some respects, it was like any other mining town he'd visited while traveling the West—but, like the others, it had touches that the others lacked. There was no church, for one thing, and no school in evidence, although the town did have a theater of sorts tucked in beside the Mother Lode saloon. Its billboard presently announced *Macbeth*, and Thorn was moved to wonder how a troupe of local actors would attack a Shakespeare play.

When it was time, he ambled down to Celestial Alley, standing across the street for some minutes and watching the Chinese at work. A maid Thorn recognized from The Pyramid stopped in for sheets at a laundry, bringing a wheelbarrow with her and piling it high. A butcher farther down the alley seemed to do brisk business, mostly chickens with their feathers plucked but heads attached, and cuts of what Thorn hoped were pork. Beyond the butcher, an apothecary dealt in herbs and powders, salves and bottles of elixir for whatever ailed his customers. The hanging signs were all illegible to Thorn, their Chinese characters appearing jagged and exotic to his Western eyes. The smells that wafted to his nostrils ranged from heavenly to horrible, mingling before they reached the thoroughfare.

At last he crossed, entered the laundry on his left, and found two men dressed all in white regarding him with frank suspicion from behind a waist-high counter. Thorn approached and gave his name, adding, "For Mr. Wu at nine o'clock."

The two men glanced at one another, then the taller of

them exited the laundry through a backdoor. Thorn waited with the other, breathing steam and bleach fumes for about five minutes, then the first man came back with another Chinese, this one in a three-piece suit and bowler hat planted squarely atop his head. The new arrival stepped around the counter, moving toward the shop's main door, and said to Thorn, "You come."

Thorn followed him, hands dangling near his holstered Colts, eyes flicking left and right, absorbing details of the narrow alleyway. As they approached a reeking slaughter-house with hogs penned up outside, Thorn's guide turned left into an open doorway and began to climb a flight of stairs. Gideon trailed him to the second floor and waited while his escort knocked and spoke outside the only door in sight.

Another voice, beyond the door, answered. Thorn's guide entered and closed the door behind him, then came back and told him, "You go in."

Thorn did as he was told, despite some trepidation, entering a kind of office-cum-storehouse with bolts of shiny cloth stacked up against one wall, another piled with crates whose contents he could not identify. Behind a spotless desk, another Chinaman stood facing him. This one was middle-aged or older, wore a round cap and a robe of sorts in matching silk, a long mustache drooping to reach his chin. Though portly, he did not appear obese. A sense of strength surrounded him, combining muscle with sheer force of personality. His voice was deep, mellifluous.

"Good morning, Mr. Thorn. Thank you for coming."

"Are you Wu Chengjun?" Gideon asked.

"I am."

"Then thanks for asking me."

"I understand," said Wu, "that you are looking for a dragon."

Randolph Boone hated residing at The Pyramid. It galled him, living under George Hearst's roof, but he was trapped, since there was no other hotel in town and he was loath to bunk with Seely Ridpath at the Belle Aire Mine. At least Hearst kept his distance, rarely pestered Boone with bids to buy his claim these days, apparently content to sit back and observe its failure from the comfort of his suite upstairs.

Bastard.

And things had gone from bad to worse.

While Boone was having breakfast in his room, avoiding any accidental contact with his rival in the restaurant below, he'd heard about the disappearance from Celestial Alley overnight, recounted by the girl who brought his food upstairs. The Chinaman who'd vanished wasn't one of Boone's former employees—or, at least, he didn't think so; who could possibly remember all their names?—but it was still a bad sign for his excavation and the camp at large.

Boone tried to picture it: a dragon swooping down over New Egypt, snatching up a human snack, then winging off into the night once more, unseen by any white man in the camp. The Chinese had been terrified, apparently, though Boone had slept through all their caterwauling with the aid of laudanum he had procured from Dr. Gilmore. Boone ostensibly consumed it to control headaches—and had, in fact, at the beginning—but he now found that the drug commanded him to drink it, and the way it made him feel was worth the asking price.

He could give up the laudanum, Boone was convinced,

if he could only get his miners back and excavate the cavern they'd discovered. He would be a rich man then, and no mistake. His find might even rival Hearst's bonanza from the Comstock Lode, put them on equal levels when it came to buying influence in Austin or in Washington, D.C.

And wouldn't that be lovely?

In the meantime, what he had was silver sitting in the ground and no one left to dig it out for him, a so-called dragon on the loose and hungry by the sound of it, while creditors kept snapping at his heels and George Hearst waited like a vulture, preening while he watched Boone's hopes circle the new flush toilet bowl located two doors from his room.

Thinking about the dragon made him think of Thorn, the young man who'd come hunting for it based on nothing but a clipping from some newspaper. Thorn emanated confidence, but that was worthless if he couldn't find the beast and deal with it before Boone found himself forced into bankruptcy. In that case, he'd be worth exactly what he'd asked for tracking down the monster: nothing.

As things stood now, Boone didn't even have the coward's option of a disappearing act. Where would he go, and how long could he live on just the money in his pocket? If his diggers came back soon enough, he'd make ends meet with silver from the cavern in his mine. But otherwise, his claim was just a busted flush and he would have to fold, take pennies on the dollar for a mine that would have made him filthy rich.

He would ride back out today, as was his habit, sit around the mine with Ridpath like old fogeys in a nursing home and talk about what might have been, or try once more to think of some solution on their own. If Thorn disappointed them, which Boone took as a given in his present state of mind, they'd need some other strategy—but what?

If the mine-dwelling monster existed but wasn't in residence now, where would they find it? And if they *could* find it, how in hell would they destroy it, bringing proof back to New Egypt that the deed was done? Boone wasn't old Saint George of English legend, slaughtering a dragon during the Crusades. He'd killed his share of snakes, and once a cougar, but beyond that he was no great hunter. Seely Ridpath was adept at potting deer and antelope to feed the miners, but he claimed he'd shot the tunnel monster more than once, with no result.

Cursing his bitter luck, Boone pushed his breakfast plate aside and reached out for the laudanum.

George Hearst was also dining in his suite, atop The Pyramid hotel. Aunt Lou had cooked one of her special ham hocks and he was enjoying it immensely when a rapping at his door distracted him. "Who is it?" he demanded.

"Cletus, Mr. Hearst."

"Enter!"

The Pinkerton came in and closed the door behind him, looking everywhere around the suite except at Hearst, turning his Stetson round and round in nervous hands.

"Out with it, Clete," Hearst said around a mouthful.

"Mr. Hearst," he said, "I wondered if you'd been apprised of last night's trouble with the Chinks?"

"What trouble, Clete?"

"Down in the alley, there. They claim something came in and snatched one of their people."

"Something? 'Came in' how?"

"Well, you know Chinks, sir."

"Do I?"

"Um, they say it was a flying dragon. Swooped down outa nowhere and made off with one of 'em."

"Not Wu Chengjun, I'm guessing."

"No, sir. No such luck."

"Nor anybody else of great importance?"

Alford blinked at that. "I didn't know there were important Chinks, sir."

"Everyone is measured on a scale. Remember that."

"Yes, sir."

"What's the reaction among the celestials?"

"Seems like they're mourning, if you can believe it. His family's shook up, I guess. The rest are doin' business just like always, but they're edgy. Passed by there myself, and some of 'em keep lookin' to the sky."

"An act, you think?" asked Hearst.

"If so, they're stickin' to it, sir. How do you read a Chink?"

"One of life's mysteries. And how's our marshal taking it?"

"Seems out of sorts. I take it he was down there last night, soon after it happened—*if* it happened—and they wouldn't tell 'im any more than I told you."

"Because that's all there is to tell, perhaps? Or are they setting up some kind of trick?"

"I couldn't rightly answer that, sir."

"No. We need someone inside that alley. Can it be arranged?" Hearst asked.

Clete frowned, shuffled his feet. "That's hard to say, sir. Chinks are clannish, don't like talkin' to the round-eyes, as they call us, if they even *can* talk proper English. Pinkerton don't have any Chinese amongst its agents that I know of. I could ask headquarters."

"Means another man sent to Fort Davis."

"For the telegraph. Yes, sir."

"And I assume the first man isn't back yet?"

"No, sir. Likely waitin' for the word on Thorn you wanted, less he's got it and he's ridin' back. I doubt they'd be that quick with it."

"The money I've been paying out," Hearst muttered to himself, "they ought to get a damn move on." And then, to Clete: "Forget about the infiltrator. Can you think of any other way to get inside their heads? Some way to find out what they're thinking, or at least what's being said among them?"

"Well, sir, there's the whores."

"Explain."

"They screw for money. Maybe one of 'em would talk for money, too. If they speak any English, that is. One of 'em might say what's goin' on along the alley, what they're up to."

"If she didn't tell her pimp first thing and feed you lies on his behalf."

"Well..."

"Who among your men would make this sacrifice?" Hearst asked.

"I got a few as might, sir. But I thought, if it's important to you, I could do the job myself."

"You did, did you?"

"Yes, sir."

"Meaning you hope I'll pay for you to have a piece of ass. See if it really goes from side to side?"

"No, sir! I'd pay the going rate myself and come right back to fill you in on details."

"Information, yes? I don't want the specifics of your *tête-à-tête* with the unfortunate, whoever she might be."

"My what, sir?"

"Never mind. Get on with it, and keep your ears pricked for whatever may be said within their hearing, if you understand a word of it."

"Yes, sir!"

Clete was turning toward the door when Hearst said, "One more thing."

"Yes, sir?"

"What is the newspaper's opinion of this incident?"

"Newspaper, sir?"

"*The Hieroglyph*." Hearst covered his exasperation, slicing off another chunk of ham.

"Well, sir, I understand the editor was down there to the alley, last night, with the marshal."

"Was she, now."

"Yes, sir. Along with Thorn, the one you asked about."

Hearst pinned his agent with a glare. "And you just thought to mention that?"

"Um..."

"Clete. The paper?"

"They ain't published yet. Comes out this afternoon, sir."

"Our marshal and the editor," Hearst said. "Are they involved?"

"Involved, sir?"

"Yes, *involved*. Romantically?"

"I don't know, sir."

"Find out before we speak again."

"Yes, sir."

"Now go and get your ashes hauled. I'm eating here."

"I am seeking the dragon," Thorn told Wu. "If it exists."

"I can assure you that it does."

"You've seen it personally?"

"No, but many of my people have. They would not lie to me."

"Because you lead the local tong?"

"Round-eyes have a misunderstanding of the tongs," Wu said. "The word initially meant 'hall' or 'meeting place.' Today, we use it to identify a brotherhood of countrymen in foreign lands, supporting one another, making life a little easier where possible."

"Unlike some of the stories that I've heard," Thorn said.

"I don't know what you've heard, nor can I be responsible for it."

"Of course." Thorn let it drop. "About the dragon..."

"Summoned from the earth," Wu said.

"By whom?"

Wu shrugged at that. "My people helped reveal it, with the *Mòxīgē rén.*"

"Which are?"

"The Mexicans, of course. Perhaps they had some reason of their own for calling up the monster."

"What I've heard," Thorn said, "they were as frightened as your people. Still are."

"Well...perhaps."

"But after this thing was released, its first attack was here, against your settlement?"

"The first attack we *know* of, Mr. Thorn. Who can predict how hungry it must be, after long ages underground?"

"Indeed." Something to think about. "Your English, Mr. Wu, is excellent."

Wu smiled, almost, and said, "How else may I communicate with round-eyes in this camp? This country? Though I do sometimes conceal it."

"You've encountered prejudice, I take it."

"From the whites, blacks, Mexicans. So far, I've had no contact with red Indians. I understand they are disdained above all others."

"Sadly, yes. By some." Thorn came back to the dragon. "In your people's legends, are these creatures normally man-eaters?"

"Legends, as you call them, from our homeland may not fit the beasts of North America," Wu said. "At home, the dragons of mythology are normally composite characters. They have a head resembling a horse's or a camel's, but with antlers like a stag, ears like a cow, and demon's eyes. Their neck and tail is like a snake's, their belly like a clam, scales like a carp, and claws much like a tiger's on their feet. Occasionally they have bat-like wings, but most do not. Unlike some European dragons, they do not breathe fire."

"And how does that stack up against the local specimen?"

"From what my people say, the witnesses, this beast is...different. It has a long head, not unlike a stork's beak. Two legs, like a bird, and not the normal dragon's four. A long neck, also like the stork's, has been reported, and great wings, but no visible feathers. And, of course, there is its massive size."

"How big?" Thorn asked. "An estimate?"

"My people mention only massive wings, some thirty, forty feet across."

More than twice the wingspan of a condor in the Andes,

three to four times that of North America's largest known bird.

"Your street outside isn't that wide," Thorn said. "When Chan Li Gong was taken—"

"You have heard his name?"

"Last night. How did the creature manage it?"

"From what I hear, it lands and folds its wings, attacks, and flies away. But, as I said, I did not witness it."

A fact Thorn now regretted, thinking Wu would make an excellent witness.

"Anything else?" he asked the tong leader.

"If your quest is successful, will you slay the creature?"

Thorn was honest when he said, "I haven't thought that far ahead."

"Be ready, Mr. Thorn. In case it comes for you."

"I'll do my best," Thorn said, Wu's beatific smile and silence indicating that their interview was over.

Walking back to his hotel, Thorn pondered what he'd learned—nothing of substance, though it was suggestive—and decided he should get another point of view. The only other people who had seen the beast so far were Mexicans, camped south of town and boycotting the Belle Aire Mine.

But would they speak to him?

Passing The Pyramid and moving toward the livery, he thought, *There's only one way to find out.*

SIX

After he'd saddled Shadow, Thorn asked for directions to the Mexican encampment, learning from the hostler that it was a half-mile south-southwest. Not far, and if his business didn't take too long, he might be back for lunch at the hotel. If not, he'd spied another restaurant between The Pyramid and Celestial Alley that promised GOOD FOOD on a sign in its window.

The ride out, at a walking pace, took seven minutes. Thorn saw the camp when he was still four hundred yards away, a settlement of tents and shacks constructed out of scraps including wood, tin, and tarpaper. Some of the shacks had stovepipes, wafting smoke from fires inside, while other misty plumes rose up from open fires. Two hundred yards and closing, Thorn saw people gathered at the outdoor fires, others roaming about on errands best known to themselves. A shifting desert breeze carried a rank aroma from the slit trench excavated forty yards due west of camp.

As Thorn approached the settlement's perimeter, three

men in peasant garb accosted him, barring his way. One of them had an old revolver tucked under the rope that served him as a belt; the other two carried machetes. Thorn reined in as one asked, "What you want, *gringo*?"

"César Estrada," he replied. "I heard from Mr. Boone that he might talk about the animal your people saw at the Belle Aire."

One of the lookouts crossed himself, all three exchanging troubled glances. Finally, the *pistolero* nodded to the fellow on his left, who turned and jogged into the camp.

"Your guns," the spokesman for the former trio said.

"What of them?"

"You must give them up to see César."

"That isn't happening," Thorn said. "Tell him my name's Gideon Thorn, and he can find me at The Pyramid in town, if he should feel like talking."

Thorn was turning Shadow toward New Egypt when the Mexican called out, "*Espere!* Wait, *señor,* until we hear what César has to say."

Thorn nodded, one hand on his saddle horn, the other on his thigh, beside the holstered right-hand Colt. He didn't think the Mexican would draw on him, but mind-reading was not among his many talents.

After what seemed like a long time but was only moments, Thorn saw the third Mexican returning, his machete still in hand. Approaching, he said something to his seeming boss in Spanish, lost on Thorn except *vienen por delante*, which he translated as "come ahead."

"All right, *gringo*," the *pistolero* said. "I take you to César."

Thorn rode Shadow, his guide walking in front of him

and glancing backward frequently, as if to verify that he was being followed. Soon they reached a hovel larger than the rest, perhaps two rooms instead of one, and Thorn dismounted, telling Shadow silently to wait for him unless a threat arose. The stallion snorted once and seemed to nod its regal head.

Thorn's escort led him to the shack's entrance, no door in evidence, and tapped his knuckles on the frame. A voice inside called out, "*Entra!*" and Thorn passed through, his armed guide lingering outside.

The shack's front room took up approximately two-thirds of its space, a rude kitchen included, on the left as Thorn entered. A small but stocky man sat at a table in the middle of the room, an empty stool directly opposite.

"*Señor* César Estrada?" Thorn inquired.

"I am Estrada. And your are...?"

"Gideon Thorn."

"Sent here by Mr. Boone."

"I've spoken to him," Thorn replied. "He didn't send me."

"And what is the difference?"

"I went to him, about the creature. He suggested you'd know more."

"Sit down." When Thorn was planted on his stool, Estrada asked, "Why do you wish to know about *Quetzalcoatl*?"

"I investigate such things. The reasons are my own."

"And yet, you come to me for help, *verdad*?"

"If you have any knowledge that could help me."

"Help you to do what, *gringo*? Find it? Kill it? Catch it for a circus like your famous P. T. Barnum's?"

"First, I want to understand it. See if it exists, in fact."

"And if it does?"

"Last night, some say the creature snatched a man from town and carried him away."

"A *chino, sí*?"

"That's what I hear."

"You care about the yellow men, *gringo*?"

"They're human beings, not a menu item for a monster."

"So, you are a *filántropo*."

"No one's ever called me a philanthropist before," Thorn said. "Some other things, but that's a new one. I investigate reports of strange, unexplained happenings."

"For reasons that you cannot say."

"Won't say, just yet."

"*Muy bien, gringo.* I tell you of *Quetzalcoatl,* and make of it what you will."

CELESTIAL ALLEY, NEW EGYPT

"You're good, Meiying," Clete Alford said, thinking, *It don't run sideways after all.* "What's your name mean in English?"

"Graceful flower," the young whore replied.

"That fits you to a tee. I wanna ask you somethin'."

"I do anything you want," she told him, smiling.

"I ain't up to it right now," he woefully admitted. "This is somethin' else."

She stared at Clete, waiting him out. At last he said, "About the dragon."

Now a shadow passed over her pale face, and she looked away from him. "Bad luck to speak of *lóng*," she said.

"That's Chinee talk for 'dragon'?" he inquired.

A jerky nod was her response.

"This ain't bad luck," he said, letting her see the Andrew Jackson fiver in his hand. Ten times the price of bedding down with him, that was. "It's all for you, not for your pimp. Just tell me what I need to know."

Meiying reached for the bill but Clete withdrew it. "Talkee first," he said.

"The *lóng* lives underground," she said.

"Used to. I know that much. What else?"

"Last night, I see it." Almost whispering.

"Tell me."

"It come from sky, like shadow falling. Chan Li Gong is feeding *zhū* at *túzǎi chǎng*."

"I didn't get that."

"Feed pigs at the slaughterhouse. Dragon comes down and take him in its jaws, flies him away."

"And where's he now?"

"Who knows?"

"Describe it for me, and you got your fiver. Better yet, *draw* it."

Clete handed her a notepad from his jacket, with a stub of pencil. Meiying took them, stuck her tongue out from a corner of her mouth as she was sketching on the paper. "Fly like bird," she said, "but no feather. Long neck, long jaw, long claws."

The drawing that she handed back to him was something Clete had never seen before, and never hoped to in his life. He traded her the Jackson for it and she tucked the bill away as he examined what she'd drawn.

It looked most like a stork, but had no tail to speak of, not even the stubby kind he'd seen on larger wading birds.

The short hind legs were almost *webbed,* and squatting in the picture, with its obviously large wings folded in on either side. The creature's neck was long, surmounted by a rounded head and long beak pointed at the end, gaping with no teeth visible.

"How big?" he asked her.

Meiying spread her arms out wide, suggesting wings. "Four times this room, mebbe."

Clete guessed the room was ten feet square and felt his stomach turn. A thing that size would dwarf an eagle, but he knew that even eagles couldn't carry off a man. Their claws weren't strong enough, much less the muscles in their necks.

"How big was this Chan fella?" he inquired.

"Come up to your shoulder, mebbe." Meiying dropped her arms and curved them, indicating girth. "But fat."

"Jesus!" Clete said, and scrambled for his trousers on the floor.

He had to get this news to Mr. Hearst, and pronto. What the boss would make of it was anybody's guess, and not Clete Alford's problem.

Not unless he had to face the monster in the drawing, somewhere down the line.

"*Quetzalcoatl* is the flying serpent, *Señor* Thorn," Estrada said. "My people worshiped it from time beyond remembering in Mexico. The Aztecs knew it as creator of mankind, a boundary-maker between earth and sky. Descriptions vary from one culture to another, but most agree it was born to the virgin *Chimalman* after the god *Onteol* appeared to her in dreams. Much like *Jesus de Nazaret* in that respect, eh?"

"Minus all the flying serpent thing," Thorn said.

"Of course. To some in Mexico, *Quetzalcoatl* was benevolent, protector of the harvest or the god of light, justice, mercy and wind. To others, it was vengeful, evil, and a man-eater. Your *chino* might agree with that, I think."

"They're leaning that way," Thorn agreed.

"Another version, which I personally find ridiculous, names *Quetzalcoatl* as Hernán Cortés, the Spaniard who destroyed the Aztecs. His arrival was disaster for the native people of my homeland, but I think he was an evil man employed by other evil men, and nothing more."

"Sounds like a safe bet," Thorn replied.

"On the other hand, some of your Mormons still believe *Quetzalcoatl* was *Jesús Cristo*, coming to North America but never mentioned in the Bible until they discovered golden tablets buried in Missouri."

"I'm not hunting Jesus," Thorn assured Estrada.

"As to *Quetzalcoatl*'s death, at least in legend, he was tricked by the god *Tezcatlipoca* into getting drunk and lying with a virgin priestess—possibly the serpent's sister *Quetzalpetlatl*. Later, sober and consumed by shame at his transgression, *Quetzalcoatl* burned himself to death as penance and his heart became the morning star."

"Well, this one isn't dead, if what I hear is true," Thorn said.

"Nor was it burned, but sleeping in the earth."

"Until the miners set it free."

"My people swear that much is true, at least," said Escobar. "The rest...well, who can say?"

"But *something* came out of the Belle Aire Mine. It's big, it flies, and can be dangerous."

"At least to the *chino*."

"And why them, if you had to guess?"

Escobar shrugged and spread his open hands. "That is beyond my reckoning."

"What did this *Quetzalcoatl* eat, aside from men?"

"The evil one took livestock, creatures of the forest, anything its greedy heart desired."

"That doesn't narrow down the field much." Thorn surmised that he would have to question local ranchers, or the marshal, to find out if any had reported missing stock.

"I ask again what you will do if you find *Quetzalcoatl*," said Estrada.

"Well, I don't work for a circus, Barnum's or whichever one you care to name. I seriously doubt that I could capture it alive, or whether that would only mean more danger to the town and everyone involved."

"So you would kill it."

"Likely, if I could. The Belle Aire's foreman claims he hit it with a rifle, more than once, and didn't bring it down."

"*Señor* Boone wants us back, and the *chino,* to help enrich him with the silver veins we found."

"You heard that, did you?"

"It is known throughout the camp. My people will not work as long as *Quetzalcoatl* might return and occupy its nest."

"It hasn't yet, if that helps. There's a watch on the Belle Aire around the clock."

"The foreman, with his mighty rifle?"

Thorn nodded. Estrada had a point. "Would you return if it was dead?"

"Why not? I know that Wu Chengjun would field his slaves."

"How's that?"

"You did not know he is a labor contractor associated with the tongs?"

"I know the tong part, or his version of it, anyway."

"The tongs recruit workers in China, bring them here, and hire them out for work on railroads, timber cutting, in the mines, wherever there is money to be made. The contractor provides their food and lodging, sometimes opium and *putas,* while he pockets all their pay and sends a portion to his masters in the old country."

"That's been illegal since the Civil War," Thorn said. "Used to be slavery. Today we call it peonage."

"And yet, it still goes on."

"Something worth looking into, once I've gotten to the bottom of this dragon business."

"You are what we call *resuelto,*" said Estrada. "Single-minded or resolved."

"I've heard it said before."

"That can be dangerous."

"I've seen that for myself."

"Yes, death has touched you. I sense that. Perhaps you wish to know why it has spared your life?"

"Are you a mind-reader?" Thorn asked.

"I have no special powers. I merely observe."

"But you can't tell me where to find *Quetzalcoatl.*"

"*Lo siento mucho, Señor* Thorn. I'm very sorry, but I can't predict the movements of a god—or of a monster."

"So it could be either one."

"Or both the same," Estrada said. "Is not our God a monster, when his wrath unfurls?"

"That's something else to think about another time," Thorn said. "Thank you for seeing me, *Señor.*"

"My pleasure. And be careful if you track the flying serpent to its lair."

THE PYRAMID HOTEL

"Aunt Lou, I'd like fried chicken for tonight," Hearst said.

"I'll put it on the menu, sir," the heavyset black woman said.

Her true name was Lucretia Marchbanks, born a slave in 1832, in Putnam County, Tennessee. Before the Civil War began, her father bought his freedom for the lordly price of seven hundred dollars, saved up over years, but she'd remained in bondage until 1863, when liberated by the president's Emancipation Proclamation. Moving on to California, she had met George Hearst, beguiled him with her culinary skills, and joined his entourage when he was on the road, searching for "color" in the hinterlands.

"And baked potato, possibly with peas?"

"No problem in the world, sir."

"You're a treasure, Lou," Hearst said, his rough hand settling for an instant on her plump shoulder.

Behind them, in the kitchen doorway, Clete Alford appeared and cleared his throat. "Excuse me, Mr. Hearst?"

"Is that a question, Clete?"

"Um...no, sir. Comin' to you with that news you asked for."

"Ah. Let's step into the dining room. It should be empty now."

It was. Hearst chose a table near the window, sat, and Alford settled opposite him, leaning forward, elbows on the table. "I did what we talked about," he said.

"Screwing the Chinese whore."

"Well, that and getting information on the creature."

"So-called creature. Tell me," Hearst commanded.

"This girl claims she saw it come down from the sky and grab a Chink, Chan something I believe his name was. Anyhow, she drew it for me."

"Drew it?"

"Yes, sir." Fishing in an inside pocket of his coat, Alford took out a notebook and presented it to Hearst. "First page, sir."

Hearst studied the sketch, frowning, turning it on its side at one point, then asked Alford, "What the hell is this?"

"A dragon's what she called it. *Lóng,* in their lingo."

"Looks like somebody plucked an egret," Hearst said.

"Yes, sir. Or a stork."

"Whatever. It's some kind of bird?"

"It flies," Clete said, "but's got no feathers. And it's *big,* o'course. *Real* big."

"How big?"

"I asked about the Chink it took. Meiying—the whore —said he's shorter'n me but stout. Whatever this thing is, it took him in its mouth or beak and flew away."

"I've seen bald eagles hunting," Hearst said. "Golden eagles, too, and red-tailed hawks. They all grab with their claws, kill with their beaks, and eat their prey while sitting on the ground unless there's danger."

"I suppose an alley fulla Chinks would qualify," Clete said.

"And when they fly, they carry what they've slaughtered in their talons, not their beaks."

"I'm only tellin' you what she said, sir."

"How big would this thing have to be, to carry off a fat celestial?"

"Meiying spread out her arms and said 'four times this room,' meaning its wingspan was around the forty-foot mark."

Hearst laughed in his face at that. "Preposterous! Insane! She had you on, Clete, in more ways than one."

"Beggin' your pardon, sir, but I don't think so. She was scared to even talk about it. Claimed it was bad luck to see this thing, much less to spread the word."

"But money changed her mind, I take it?"

"Just a fiver."

"Which she'll hand directly to her pimp."

"I said she didn't have to."

"Oh, well *that* makes all the difference." Hearst paused in his derision, took another long look at the sketch, and asked, "You take her seriously, then?"

"Within her limits, sir."

"Meaning?"

"Well, she's a Chink, and she's a whore."

"Of course. But still a *sighted* Chinese whore, although she took you to her crib."

Missing the dig, Alford said, "Right. Yes, sir."

"So she was either lying for the five-spot or she wasn't, and you'd vote for truth."

"I would, sir."

"Bet your job on it?"

That made Clete hesitate, but he replied, at last, "Yes, sir. Whatever Meiying told me, *she* believed it."

"Fair enough. And if this thing exists, we still have no idea what it might be."

"Unless it *is* a dragon, sir."

"Unless that." Handing back the notebook, Hearst said, "Very well, Clete. Head back to the Silver Crown. I'll be there sometime after lunch, to have a look around."

"Yes, sir."

Alone, still seated at the window table, Hearst considered what he'd heard. A living dragon didn't fit in his world, his cosmology, where precious metals dominated the affairs of men. If such beings were real, it might change everything.

More reason to destroy it.

And for that, more reason to find out what role Gideon Thorn played in the hunt.

SEVEN

NEW EGYPT

Thorn dropped Shadow at the livery, got him unsaddled, watched the hostler brush the stallion down after his ride out to César Estrada's camp, and checked on Bell before he walked back to The Pyramid. He barely made a half-block from the stable when a female voice called out to him and he saw Angelina Farnum hurrying across the thoroughfare.

"I looked for you at the hotel," she said, by way of greeting.

"I was out," Thorn answered.

"So I see. Pursuing your investigation?"

"In a nutshell."

"That's a shell I'd like to crack. You still owe me an interview, if you recall. Some *quid pro quo.*"

"Are journalists always this pushy?" Thorn inquired, smiling. He knew the answer from experience.

"The good ones are," she said. "And I'm a good one."

"Sorry, but I haven't read your paper yet."

"That's fine. I want you *in* it, not just reading it."

"Why me?"

"Because you're interesting, Mr. Thorn. I've never heard of anybody else who rides around the West investigating random mysteries."

"Not random," he corrected her. "The ones that interest me and lead me closer to my goal."

"Which is?"

"I don't mind telling you, but at the moment I'm a little busy. Are you free for dinner? We could meet at the hotel. I recommend their chef."

"Aunt Lou," said Angela. "She's good, all right. And works for Mr. Hearst, the hotel's owner."

"Not to mention all his mining interests, the Silver Crown among them."

"You're aware of him, I see."

"We've met, in fact."

"Oh, yes? How did that come about?"

"He asked me how I liked my dinner—and about my interest in the local dragon stories."

"Ah."

"So you and he appear to have something in common."

"Oh?"

"Picking my brain."

"He's doing more than that," she said.

"Meaning?"

"Word has it that he's sent one of his Pinkertons to Fort Davis. They have a telegraph. His man's supposed to contact headquarters and find out what he can about your background, motives for your presence in New Egypt, anything the Eye That Never Sleeps can learn about you."

"No law against it, I suppose," Thorn said, forcing another smile.

"There ought to be, but no. There isn't."

"Should I ask how you obtained this information?"

"I'm a journalist, remember? I have sources. Eyes and ears in the community."

"Which you cannot reveal?"

"Strictly unethical."

"In that case, thank you for the warning."

Gideon could not imagine any way for Hearst to damage him by simply rooting through the details of his life. The fortune he'd inherited was safe and sound, protected by the legal firm of Messrs. Block, Enright and Thorn in Boston, and his stately home on Beacon Hill was guarded by Obi Magoro, Thorn's friend and first tutor from his childhood, born in Africa, refined dramatically in service to the Thorns, but still selectively ferocious in his latter years.

"How do you get along with Randolph Boone?" she asked.

"We've also met."

"And?"

"Are you asking me to guess at what he's thinking? What he may or may not do about the mine?"

"You know Hearst wants it."

"What I hear," Thorn said, "he wants *all* mines, all claims. He's after 'color,' anywhere, at any price, by any means."

"You're not a great admirer, then," she said.

"I have no quarrel with any honest businessman. Even the shady ones draw lines they normally won't cross."

"Some do. The so-called robber barons have a reputation for annihilating any competition, bending workers to their will by violence, breaking the law whenever it fulfills their needs."

"I'm not a lawman or a prosecutor," Thorn reminded her.

"No. At the moment, you're a dragon hunter."

"Are you trying to advance the interview?"

"Advance it?"

"Dinner, at The Pyramid. We'll talk then, and I'll tell you what I can."

"Hedging already?"

"I believe that everyone has secrets, most of which are not the public's business or concern. Ergo--"

"*Ergo?*"

"They teach English at Harvard, among other things." Thorn pressed ahead. "Ergo, a journalist has no legitimate concern with any facts that don't affect the public or the body politic."

"Not even human interest?"

"I doubt sincerely whether many of New Egypt's residents have any burning interest in me."

"You'd lose that bet," she said. "You're all the rage with local gossips in the know—or, rather, those who *think* they know."

Thorn smiled again at that, not forcing it this time. "We'll see, if you accept my invitation."

"Very well. But strictly business," she reminded him, a twinkle in her eye belying it.

"Of course," Thorn said, and watched her cross the street, back toward her office.

Randolph Boone was getting ready for his daily ride out to the Belle Aire Mine when knocking on his door distracted him from buttoning his trouser fly. He finished, moved to crack the door, and was surprised to find George Hearst upon the threshold, peering in at him.

"My rent's paid up," Boone said. "What do you want?"

"A civil word," Hearst said, "if that's agreeable."

Reluctantly, Boone stood aside, then checked the corridor for lurking Pinkertons before he closed it.

"I don't normally have bodyguards inside my own hotel," Hearst said.

"These aren't what I'd call normal times," said Boone.

"This dragon business, you're referring to."

"For starters."

"It appears to have an appetite for Chinese food," said Hearst.

"You find that humorous?"

"I'm not inclined to weep about it. Nor should you, since they're not working for you anymore."

"I'll ask again: what do you want?"

"Same thing I've always wanted, Randolph. Name a price. Get out from under your disaster of a claim."

"If it's such a disaster, why the interest?"

"That's my concern."

"And mine, if you would have me sell it to you."

"I'm acquisitive by nature," Hearst replied. "And where the color is concerned, I'm something of a gambler. Just because you've failed to make the Belle Aire pay, it doesn't mean I will."

"And who says that I've failed?" asked Boone.

"You have no miners left. Your foreman sits out there alone, watching the sky for monsters from a children's story. What would you call it?"

Boone nearly spat the truth at Hearst, about the massive silver vein found in the cavern where the beast, whatever it might be, had lain concealed, but even as he bit his tongue, he guessed that Hearst already knew the truth. He wanted to be richer still, to lord it over New Egypt, and now he hoped to squeeze Boone out before the Belle Aire before Boone's strike placed them upon an equal level.

"I would call it wishful thinking on your part," Boone said. "And I decline your offer."

"But you haven't heard it yet."

"I heard the others. None of them impressed me."

"You're a stubborn man, Randolph."

"Spoken by one who knows."

"The difference between us is that I'm *successful,* while you're floundering. I have the necessary workers to complete a task."

"And your own private army standing by."

"You think I've come to threaten you?"

Boone mulled that over for a moment, then replied, "I doubt you threaten anyone directly, on your own account. Perhaps a whisper in the ears of little men, when no one else is listening. Beyond that, I imagine you just point your Pinkertons like guns and let them do the dirty work. You pay lawmen, judges and politicians to behave like monkeys: see no evil, hear no evil, speak no evil."

"I am quite the Devil in your mind," said Hearst.

"*A* devil, possibly. I draw the line at naming you as Lucifer himself."

"That's something, anyway. About my offer..."

"Keep it to yourself. The answer's 'no,' regardless of the bankroll in your pocket."

"As a rule, I never carry cash myself."

"Letting someone else settle the bills. A good way to stay rich."

"I understand you hate and fear me, Randolph."

"Well, you're half right."

Hearst chuckled at that, a harsh sound, as of gravel in a sifter. "I admire a man who keeps his sense of humor while he's drowning."

"Only treading water," Boone replied. "And waiting for my second wind."

"It seems to be a long time coming, but I trust that you know best what's good for you and for your heirs. A son out in Los Angeles, if I am not mistaken, living with his mother since the two of you divorced."

"And now the mention of my family."

"Ex-family?"

"You're so predictable," Boone said. "A bully always is."

"Do you feel bullied, Randolph? If I've played some part in that, unwittingly, I'm happy to apologize."

Boone walked back to the door and opened it. "Why don't you tell your story walking, *George*."

"Your funeral," Hearst said, then hesitated on the threshold. "That's a mere figure of speech, you understand. Watching you flail about and try to save a busted mine is so pathetic for the rest of us."

Boone closed the door on Hearst and locked it, swallowing the epithets he longed to hurl after the gloating bastard.

But I'm not drowned yet, he thought, fists clenched. *Not yet.*

Angelina Farnum took a wicker basket filled with issues of *The Hieroglyph* and left her operator to his work while she went out to leave copies at various establishments in town that helped her sell the newspaper. Six copies for The Pyramid to start, one for the manager, the rest distributed among his paying guests as complementary rewards for staying at New Egypt's sole hotel, and that stop made her think of Gideon, their dinner meeting scheduled for that evening.

Some townsfolk took for granted that she was "involved" with Seth Rockwell, a misconception that the marshal seemed to share, suffering silent injury each time she put him in his proper place. As far as Angelina was concerned, the two of them were friends and colleagues—a reporter always needed contacts in the field of law enforcement—but it went no further. They were not a couple, secretly or otherwise, no matter what the gossips thought, but how could she defeat the rumors, short of taking out a front-page editorial?

With Thorn now, there was *something*, but she couldn't put her finger on it. He was quiet, gentlemanly, and mysterious. His quest, which she hoped to unravel for herself and for her audience, intrigued her. How and why had he begun to roam the West, pursuing monsters or their shadows? Why was George Hearst driven to spend money searching out the details of Thorn's past?

For that, she'd have to ask the mining king, and she was not prepared to do that at the present time. Her own research on Hearst had taught her how he dealt with people that annoyed him. On the legal side of things, he drove them out of business, setting up a rival bank, store, assay office, or a newspaper to undersell his enemies and leave them destitute. On the *il*legal side...well, that was rumor and beyond her purview as a reputable journalist.

But if she wound up fighting for her economic life, perhaps she'd change her mind.

First, Thorn. She rarely handled anyone with kid gloves —grieving widows or the victims of a natural disaster, possibly—but otherwise she asked straightforward questions and expected honest answers. That did not require combativeness, in most cases. She kept her stern face in reserve, for those occasions when a wall of silence was erected to defeat her and to harm the public interest. With Gideon, a private man by all appearances, she thought a softer touch might do the trick.

Not *that* soft, certainly, but showing some consideration to a man she barely knew.

Her front-page story on the vanishing of Chan Li Gong would light a fire under New Egypt. Some readers would scoff at it, others would worry, most would simply wonder what was happening, but with a hint of apprehension in their minds. If there *was* some new predator at large, winging across the night skies overhead, which one of them was truly safe?

And if it were a hoax, perhaps with murder cast in a supporting role, who was responsible?

Objective truth was Angelina's goal as a reporter. Filtering the human side of things was often difficult, removing just enough of the emotion from a story so that it was clarified, without becoming dull and colorless, was her eternal challenge.

She suspected Gideon could help with that—or, at the very least, impart a fresh dimension to New Egypt's mystery. Whether the dragon was a living thing or not, its very name had drawn him here, away from other riddles waiting to be solved.

She thought about his pistols, wondered if he'd ever used them, and suppressed a shiver that came over her despite the morning's heat. When they sat down to eat that night, and she began to question him, she was the hunter, Thorn her prey.

And if she snared him, what would be the end result for either one of them?

SILVER CROWN MINE

George Hearst rode out alone to view his claim, driving a trap he'd rented from the livery, drawn by an amber champagne gelding. He had no fear of assassination there, but wore a pistol tucked beneath his vest, a Beaumont-Adams double-action six-shooter presently used by British army officers, chambered for .442-caliber Webley center-fire cartridges. Hearst was proficient in its use but had not personally shot a man with that or any other gun.

He delegated such behavior to his minions, chiefly Pinkertons.

Arriving at the mine on schedule, Hearst saw Clete Alford coming out to meet him. Other gunmen kept a sharp eye on the Cornish miners trundling in and out with cars and wheelbarrows of ore and backfill, dumping waste in pits, transporting silver-bearing stone to the stamp mills where it was crushed for further processing. A Pinkerton lounging behind the big brass Gatling gun watched over all, as if expecting hostile Indians or an invasion by some Mongol horde.

"Good morning, sir," Clete greeted him. "All runnin' smoothly here, no sign of any dragons."

Hearst ignored the poor attempt at jocularity and stepped down from the trap. "Have someone tend the horse," he said.

"Yes, sir!"

While Alford went to carry out that order, Hearst

walked to a shack close by the Silver Crown's adit, and barged in without knocking. Otis Breen, his manager on-site, looked up from paperwork and muttered, "Morning, George," first-name familiarity permitted by their years together on the Comstock Lode and other claims.

"How goes it?" Hearst inquired.

"It's good. We're proving out and doing well. It's not as rich as what we hear about the Belle Aire, mind you, but we'll turn a tidy profit."

"Tidy," Hearst echoed, as if the term offended him.

"The word I'd use."

"While Boone is sitting on a goddamn mother lode and won't consider selling out."

"Would you?"

"If I was thwarted from extracting it, I might."

"The hell you would. We both know better."

"Well..."

"What did you offer him?"

"It's immaterial. He's made it clear that he won't sell to me at any price."

"Is that the end?"

"For him."

"You put it to him just that way?"

"Course not. You think I'm going simple?"

"Never have and never will," Breen said. "He has no partners, just the family in California."

"I might have mentioned them."

"I see."

"He took offense."

"As you would, in his place."

"He has a way of getting on my nerves."

"Because he won't hand over what you want."

Hearst felt his shoulders slump. "You know me too damn well, Otis."

"Just well enough."

"How are the Cornish holding up."

"They do their work. A couple of them have been raising union talk again."

"Let Alford have their names."

"Already done. It's Chenoweth and Glasson. I have their replacements standing by."

"I'll never understand why men can't just be happy with their wages."

"Like you were, before the strike at Sutter's Mill?"

"I'm different," Hearst said.

"All men want more. Most aren't equipped to grab it and hang on."

"Their problem."

"And yours maybe, if the climate ever changes back in Washington."

"Grant's whole administration is a sinkhole of corruption. If he doesn't run again next year, whoever takes his place will be the same."

"We hope."

"A true reformer only makes it to the top by accident, once in a lifetime," Hearst replied. "Nobody gets that far on purpose by refusing compromises, turning down the bribes. Forget about love songs. It's money makes the world go 'round."

"You've got that covered, then."

"About the Cornish. Are they worried over dragons and the like?"

"There's been some talk about it," Breen replied. "The English have their stories, too. Some saint of theirs supposedly killed one, a long time back."

"His name was George, the same as mine," Hearst said.

"Well, maybe that will put their minds at ease, together with the Gatling gun."

"No talk of walking out, then?"

"Not over a flying monster. When we're shed of Chenoweth and Glasson it should slack off for another while."

"Right. Give the go-ahead."

"You didn't want to do it?"

"Are you testing me?"

"I wouldn't dream of it," Otis replied.

EIGHT

THE PYRAMID HOTEL

Thorn descended at the stroke of six o'clock, pleased to find Angelina Farnum just arriving off the street. He greeted her and pressed her hand briefly—no shake, no knuckle kiss—and stood beside her while the waitress grabbed two menus, steering them off to the left, a window table in the northeast corner of the dining room. Thorn seated Angela and sat across from her, his back against the wall.

"You're punctual," he said.

"A recommended trait for journalists."

"No eagerness involved?"

"To get your story down on paper? Absolutely, Mr. Thorn."

His flirting skills nearly exhausted, he replied, "Please call me Gideon."

"If you will call me Angela."

"Agreed."

The waitress recognized them both as customers who knew their way around the dinner menu at The Pyramid.

Angela ordered an appetizer, oyster stew, and followed it with half a broiled chicken, with baked potato on the side and peas cooked with pearl onions. Thorn made it unanimous and asked for coffee to accompany his meal, while Angela ordered white wine.

"Prompt, confident, and, I suspect, an eater," Thorn suggested.

"Guilty. Are you one of those who likes his women rail-thin, eating like a bird?"

"*Not* guilty, but it hardly matters," he replied. "You're not my woman."

"No. I'm still my own and happy with my lot in life." Her eyes kept coming back to Gideon's uncovered scalp, the white steak running like a part from his hairline, back to the crown. She nodded toward it, asking, "Is it rude of me to ask?"

"The obvious?" He shook his head, adding, "No, not at all."

"Well, then?"

"No notebook?"

"It would draw attention. I'll remember accurately."

"Well, it's tied in with the reason why I travel now," he said. "When I was two years old, in Kansas Territory—now a part of Colorado, fronting on the eastern Rockies—something killed my parents and my older brother."

"Something?" She was leaning forward slightly, possibly involuntarily.

"The local lawman blamed a grizzly, but the season was all wrong, the fragments of my memory dispute it, and the thing was never found alive or dead."

"That's terrible! And you...oh, God, you hunt it still?"

"In my own way. After I went back east to school, it

finally occurred to me that anytime officials cover up a crime, it has significance."

"Why Texas, then, instead of Kansas—I mean Colorado."

"Oh, I've been back to the old homestead. My first stop, but it was demolished, nothing left to jog my brain or put me on the track."

"So you chase other monsters. Hoping..."

"That I'll find a pattern and discover something useful. Or, at least, relieve some other families still waiting for an answer on what happened to their loved ones."

"Did you *see* the creature, all those years ago?"

"I did, and it looked something like a bear. Larger and heavier, yet faster, out and roaming in the snow when grizzlies and the smaller bears should have been holed up in their caves. I may be lying to myself, but I don't think it was a bear. I still believe that it was...something else."

"And left its mark on you," she said.

"More than a scar," said Gideon. "Instead of ripping off my scalp or head entirely, one claw barely creased the skin, and what I got was this white blaze. No bald spot, no lost hair that didn't soon grow back. I can't explain it, but I think I'm meant to find it somehow, someday."

"Not a dragon, though."

"No, ma'am. There's no comparison."

"And yet, you're here."

"Investigating something that may open up before my eyes and grant me understanding, or snap shut and leave me in the dark again."

"This time you're caught between two factions bent on drawing silver from the earth."

"That is a complication," Thorn replied. "And one of those involved is seated by the kitchen door."

Angela turned her head, saw Randolph Boone having the chicken on his own, taking one seat at a table for two, and faced back toward Gideon Thorn.

"He could lose everything, I think," she said. "Hearst nearly has him down and hogtied."

"Nothing's over till the last gun sounds," Thorn told her.

"Which reminds me. You're wearing your Colts to dinner in what passes for the poshest restaurant in New Egypt."

"Nobody seems disturbed," he said, peering around the room.

"They're all too busy looking at your hair."

That nearly made Thorn laugh, but he contained it, asking, "What else shall we talk about?"

Randolph Boone was eating his half-chicken with a knife and fork, leaving the yokels to dismember theirs with greasy fingers. He had seen Gideon Thorn come down for dinner and was mildly startled when Thorn met *The Hieroglyph*'s publisher coming off the thoroughfare and sat with her, a window seat. Boone wondered what they had to talk about, whether there was a spark between them, and decided that he didn't care.

He had more pressing things to think about.

Boone loved the food Aunt Lou prepared for diners at The Pyramid, but hated giving credit for it to a hanger-on of George Hearst, who was breathing down his neck and wouldn't rest until he got his clutching fingers on the Belle Aire Mine. That struggle had not surfaced openly at first, but now that Boone was down—not out, but maybe on his way—the knives were out.

I won't sell to him, Boone repeated silently, while working nonstop on his meal. *I'd rather dynamite the shaft and build a house on top of it.*

Make that a small one, since he wouldn't have much money left. And even then, how long before starvation ran him off and Hearst laid claim to what he'd found, bringing more Cornish in to open up the mine anew and reap his rich reward?

The only winning hand that Boone had left was getting back his Mexican and Chinese miners, pressing on into the earth—and that meant proving to both sides that he, or someone else, had slain the dragon that was terrifying them. They had to *see* it dead, convince themselves that no danger remained. But who would do the deed and save Boone from the spreading wings of bankruptcy that hovered over him?

He glanced across the dining room toward Thorn once more, the man in black with a peculiar streak of white shot through his black hair, leaning forward, telling Angelina Farnum something Boone could not decipher from Thorn's moving lips. Whatever he was saying, Thorn appeared to have her totally in thrall.

When he was younger, Boone had had a similar effect on certain women. Those who valued money and adventure were amused to hear his tales of mining in the rough camps and the boomtowns, spotting color when it slipped past lesser men and wound up in Boone's bank account. He'd never been on par with George Hearst when it came to wealth, but he had done all right and meant to do a damn sight better, till a lizard down a mineshaft ruined him.

Boone looked around for Hearst, hoping he wouldn't

wander through the dining room and stop to gloat again or drop another offer for the Belle Aire on his table. So far, Hearst had fudged the price upward a little bit each time, temptation knocking, but Boone knew the offered price would soon start dropping. Every day Boone's miners stayed away, although the value of his strike remained static, Boone's cash was bleeding out.

And soon there would be nothing left.

He thought about evacuating, leaving town without a word to Hearst or anybody else around New Egypt, keep them wondering where he had gone and when they'd hear from him again. The law required a month or so of searching, before agents of the territory deemed his claim abandoned and it went to auction with a surefire sale to Hearst. By then, Boone could be...where?

He'd picked up rumors of a gold strike somewhere in the Black Hills of Dakota Territory, not too far from Deadwood. There was trouble with the Sioux, of course, since signing of the Yankton Treaty that had ceded most of the southeastern territory to the U.S. government, but even is a war broke out sometime, Boone could be in on the ground floor of gold mining in the Badlands. He had cash enough to pull it off, barely, and while he hated being run off from a claim like the Belle Aire, he didn't want to die, either.

Not this way, as a failure.

Blow the shaft and then *head out,* he though, smiling over his dinner as he ate.

Or think about it, anyway.

And maybe, while he thought about it, Thorn would prove to be a dragon-slayer after all.

"So tell me, Gideon, how many incidents or situations—cases?—have you solved do far?"

He smiled across the table, gray eyes looking deep into her green ones. Angelina felt a tickle there and made a silent vow to keep her mind on business.

"That depends on what you mean by 'solved'," he said. "I'm coming up on twenty mysteries so far that interested me."

"That many?"

"Several of them proved to have completely natural solutions. Someone glimpsed an animal but didn't know *what* they were seeing. Weather lends itself to others, tricks of light or wind. A few were outright hoaxes, someone dressing up or making funny tracks to scare the neighbors, and it just gets out of hand."

"No deep, abiding riddles then?" she asked.

"I wouldn't go that far. Some of the jobs involve a crime, or more than one. Last month, in Tularosa—"

"That's New Mexico?" she interrupted him.

"Correct. They had a string of murders, not the best to talk about over a meal. Turned out one of the locals had gone *loco,* dressed up in a bear's skin, claws and all, with wolf's teeth in his mouth to maul folks, mostly when there was a full moon in the sky."

"I heard something about that, but I never got the details. Was it horrible? How did you stop him, finally?"

"I shot him," Thorn replied, and speared another piece of chicken on his fork.

"Your pistols aren't for show, then," Angelina said, watching him eat.

"They come in handy now and then," he granted.

"But up against the Pinkertons..."

"That's not my game."

"What makes you think you'll have a choice?"

"My only interest in the Belle Aire Mine is what came out of it, and where that creature—call it what you will—is hiding out right now."

"Waiting to strike again?"

Thorn shrugged. "We shouldn't be surprised. If it's a living thing, it has to eat, like every other creature on God's earth."

"Speaking of God, are you religious Mr. Thorn?"

"I've studied all the main beliefs, some of the smaller ones besides, but haven't fastened onto one as yet."

"So, not a praying man?"

"I never saw a need for it. What others do is up to them. Yourself?"

"There's no church in New Egypt," Angelina said, dodging the question.

"People pray wherever they're inclined to," he replied. "Working the fields, building a barn, riding from town to town. At least, that's what I hear."

"You have no fear of supernatural events?" she asked.

"I haven't seen one yet, far as I know," Thorn said. "There've been some things I can't explain right now, but I'm still working on them."

"And what about your family? Is their fate destined to remain unknown?"

"I don't presume to interfere with destiny, whatever that is. They're all gone, my family. I can't change that. But have I given up on solving it? Not yet."

They had cleaned their plates by now, and when the waitress came around again they both passed on dessert, although the rhubarb pie was tempting. Angelina had the information that she needed for a good, insightful story on the stranger in New Egypt's midst that would illuminate his presence and his purpose to her readers. Now...

"I should be going," she told Thorn. "It's not fair to monopolize your time."

"It's dark out," he observed. "How are the streets this time of night?"

"About the same as any other time. We take our chances."

"Then I'll walk you home."

"That really isn't—" She was going to say *necessary,* but he cut her off.

"My pleasure. I could use a stretch, after that meal."

Thorn paid, waved off her effort to contribute, and they left the hotel restaurant together, turning north along the thoroughfare toward Angelina's boarding house.

"I live at Mrs. Hilstrom's," she informed him. "Very strict on curfew, but she likes *The Hieroglyph* and makes exceptions if I tell her in advance I'm working late."

"Like living with your parents."

"In a way. She keeps a hawk eye out for men lurking around the house."

"You get a lot of that?"

She was about to say *not much,* when Angelina blinked and said, "Oh, damn!" instead.

"What's wrong?" Thorn asked.

"It's Seth."

Seth Rockwell walked his beat along the thoroughfare, occasionally glancing at the sky and half expecting giant wings, swooping to snatch him up or wheeling toward

Celestial Alley. He would look in on the Chinese soon, but drew the line at riding out of town to check César Estrada's Mexicans. Let Randolph Boone do that, if he was so inclined.

New Egypt's leading citizens, through comments passed along to Rockwell in the last few days, had strongly urged him to resume nighttime patrols, a practice he'd abandoned after taking down three burglars who had tried to blow the bank's safe on a Tuesday night and make off with deposits, both in cash and silver. Seth had tried his best to take them peaceably, but they'd insisted on a fight, two of them dying at his hand, the third a wheelchair cripple now, locked up at Huntsville, with another seven years remaining on the sentence he would likely never finish out alive.

Walking the beat was fine with Rockwell. He'd been gaining weight the past few months, enjoying Aunt Lou's cooking more than he did exercise, and Seth thought that had hurt his prospects with the widow Farnum. She'd come to New Egypt with her husband, helping with *The Hieroglyph,* and saw him die crossing the street one morning, when a team of horses bolted with its wagon. After planting him, instead of giving up and going back to Kansas City, Angelina stayed to keep the paper going, doing better than her husband ever had at selling ads.

Rockwell admired that, her determination—and she wasn't hard to look at, either, truth be told. The problem was his nerve, or lack of same, where women were concerned. Seth did all right with hookers, cut and dried with an exchange of cash for services, but building a relationship was different. He hadn't really gotten off the ground with Angelina yet, and—

Here she comes, he thought, startled, heading directly toward him on the wooden sidewalk, east side of the thoroughfare. And she was walking with the stranger dressed in black, Gideon Thorn.

What's that about? Seth wondered. And decided that, while it might seem intrusive, even rude, he had to know.

The widow Farnum and her escort slowed as he approached. Seth saw that they weren't holding hands, and her arm wasn't looped through Thorn's. Good signs. He called to them from thirty feet: "Miz Farnum. Mr. Thorn. What brings you out this evening?"

"Taking the air," said Angelina, while Thorn held his peace. "And you?"

"Routine patrol before I head back home."

"Not dragon hunting?" Angelina teased.

"I haven't seen one yet and don't expect to," Rockwell said.

"But Chan Li Gong—"

"Is missing, so the Chinks say."

"Seth!" Her tone hit Rockwell like a splash of ice-cold water.

"Sorry, Angelina. No affront to the celestials intended."

"They're *Chinese,* for heaven's sake!" she scolded him.

Dropping the subject, Rockwell turned to Thorn and left her fuming. "What about you? Any dragon sightings?"

"None so far," Thorn said, "but there's still."

Seth turned back to Angelina, asked her, "Working on a story?"

"Having dinner," she said coolly. Was that a defensive tone?

"A social outing, then."

"Is something wrong, Seth?" she inquired.

"Nothin' at all," he said, smiling from ear to ear. "Have a good night, you two. I'm still a workin' man."

With that, he left them on the sidewalk, never looking

back to see how they were taking it. Right now, Seth didn't care if Angelina hated him or not. She would get over it when Thorn left town, whenever that might be. No guarantee she would have thawed toward Seth by then, of course. Some women—*most* women, if he were being honest with himself—saw little in him to attract them, from his long face and his gangly form to his low-paying job.

I should've been a miner, Rockwell thought, *chasing the color or the dream of it, moving in circles where things happened fast and brought hefty rewards.*

Most times, of course, a miner didn't strike it rich.

He only got the shaft.

NINE

SILVER CROWN MINE

Otis Breen was working late, not an unusual circumstance. The Silver Crown ran double shifts, twelve hours each, one crew eating and sleeping while the other toiled below ground in the ever-dark, where lamps provided smoky, noxious light around the clock. Breen normally stayed at his post till eight p.m. or so, if there was no emergency, recording tonnage shifted, checking on the stamp mills— Mr. Hearst was running two so far, hoping to add a third— and assaying the ore extracted. Guard duty fell to the Pinkertons. Only in dire emergency would Breen venture into the shaft.

This Wednesday night, his first hint of a crisis at the Silver Crown was shouting from the Cornish, quickly turning into screams. Breen hesitated, setting down his pencil, reaching for the top drawer of his small desk where he kept an Apache revolver when it was not tucked into his pocket.

Should he leave his nest and find out what was happening, or let the trouble come to him?

First thing, Breen opened the Apache. First designed in Belgium, it was quirky but appealed to him—a double-action pinfire revolver, no barrel beyond the cylinder containing six .27-caliber rounds, which reduced its range to point-blank firing. The weapon's handle was a folding knuckleduster, useful for a beating if the cylinder was clutched inside one's palm. Below the cylinder, a two-inch "bayonet" folded against the pistol's frame, snapped open with depression of a button to become a stabbing tool.

The piece was small, easy to hide, and suited Otis Breen, whose eyes behind thick lenses weren't the best in any light.

Clutching the pistol, Breen rose from his desk and started toward the doorway of his shack-cum-office, more screams rising now. When he was halfway to the exit, gunfire echoed from the dark outside and froze him in his tracks.

Christ! Were the miners in revolt?

There'd been some muttering among the Cornish, always was and always would be, but the Pinkertons eliminated union agitators when they showed their colors, making it look like an accident or drunken fight in town. Otis had never worked a Hearst mine where the agitation turned to mayhem on the workers' part, and couldn't figure what had driven this group to the sticking point without more warning in advance.

Although he was Hearst's manager, Breen didn't deal with that side of the mining industry. Still, if a riot was erupting, he could hardly sit it out, hiding inside his quarters, hoping that the rebels wouldn't come for him. Trembling, he gripped the door's knob, opened it, and stepped outside—into a scene of chaos.

Men were running to and fro around the adit, more emerging from the miners' bunkhouse where they slept in shifts, one set of sagging bunks sufficing for the lot. The Pinkertons were paying no attention to the workers, rather aiming firearms toward the sky and firing volleys that seemed pointless, as if they were just now celebrating Independence Day.

By daylight, Breen would probably have seen the swooping shadow. As it was, full dark except for lamps and torches placed around the adit and the stamp mills, he saw nothing till a huge winged form swept past him, skimming low over the field and toppling men to left and right. Its dangling feet had talons, Breen could see that much, and as it veered away from him the flying nightmare grabbed one of the Pinkertons, lifting him up, up, and away.

The man screamed, long and loud, the volume of his protest swiftly dwindling in the distance. Breen stared after the unfortunate and his abductor, soon lost them, then saw the great wings slowly flapping as they crossed the half disc of the pale third quarter moon.

When beast and man were clearly out of range, the gunfire faltered, then died off completely. Otis Breen stood dumbstruck on the threshold of his hut, wondering what in hell he was supposed to tell the boss.

Clete Alford stumbled toward him then, asking in parrot fashion, "Did you see it? Did you see it?"

Breen nodded dumbly, then managed to say, "You'd better saddle up and go tell Mr. Hearst."

NEW EGYPT

Seth Rockwell had his boots and gunbelt off, was working on his trousers, when a pounding on his front door made him groan. He clumped out of the bedroom in his stocking feet, across the little parlor, shouting to the unknown caller, "Hold your horses!"

It was Bobby Ward, one of his deputies, red-faced and out of breath from running. "Marshal!" he gasped out. "Come quick! The Chinks is all riled up again."

"And you can't handle it?"

"I reckon not. Todd's down there now, but they won't listen to 'im, jabberin' the way they do."

Todd Glanton was the marshal's other full-time deputy. They took the night shift in rotation, two men on, one off, and this should have been Rockwell's night to rest.

"You disappoint me," Seth told Ward, watching the young man's face sag. "Wait here till I'm dressed."

He closed the door on Ward, went back to don his boots and pistol belt, his hat, the vest that bore his badge. When he had pulled himself together, Rockwell exited the house and locked the door behind him, then told Ward, "Show me."

The walked down to Celestial Alley, Rockwell stolidly resisting Ward's plea that they run, arriving there some ten minutes after Seth first heard the knocking on his door. Ward had it right, as far as the Chinese went. They were stirred up good and proper, raising singsong hell and going every which way, staying clear, as far as Seth could tell, from the far end around the slaughterhouse.

"What now?" he asked Todd Gant.

"Beats me," the deputy replied. "They won't let me go down there, just keep clamorin' for you."

"Todd, you're a white man with a badge and gun. What do you mean, they wouldn't let you pass?"

"Well, hell, I wasn't gonna *shoot* 'em over it."

Seth shook his head and brushed past Glanton, headed for the alley's crowded mouth. Ahead of him, Wu Chengjun eased through ranks of agitated Asians, saying, "Marshal here at last. This not our fault."

"*What's* not your fault?" Rockwell demanded.

"Dead man. Fall from sky."

"Show me," Seth said.

Wu led him through the alley, Chinese parting as if Wu were Moses crossing the Red Sea. They reached the hog pen, passed it, then Seth's escort stopped and pointed to the ground.

"Is that—?" Seth caught himself before he finished, swallowed back the question.

At first glance, he hadn't thought it was a body—and, in truth, it wasn't. Not a whole one, anyway. The man, whoever he had been, was missing head, shoulders and arms, as if his upper body had been torn or sawn off at the armpits, right across his chest. The part that fell to earth—small doubt about the drop, considering the bloody splash he'd made on impact—was the rest of him, torso and all beneath it, with his boots and gunbelt still in place.

"Somebody take his pistol?" Rockwell asked.

"Nobody touch," Wu said. "My people not take gun."

"All right," Rockwell replied, deciding that it wasn't worth an argument. He turned to Bobby Ward and said, "Fetch Millard Gilmore and Isaiah Kent."

"Yes, sir!"

Seth wasn't sure New Egypt's undertaker had experience with severed corpses, but there had been mining accidents before that left men badly mangled in their wake. Before this partial stiff was boxed, he wanted Doc Gilmore, the town's only physician, to examine it and try to guess the cause of death.

What tore a man in half, then dropped him from the sky?

Jesus, thought Rockwell, *please don't let it be a flying dragon.*

But his next best guess was...nothing.

If the dead man wasn't picked up somewhere else, slaughtered, and then transported here, Rockwell had no other ideas.

"Shouldn't be long, now," he told Wu. "We'll get this mess out of your way and you can go ahead, doin' whatever you-all do.

"*Lóng,*" someone muttered, close behind Rockwell, and it caught on, making the rounds in frightened whispers.

"They say 'dragon'," Wu translated for him.

"Never seen one and I never hope to," Rockwell said, still staring at the partial corpse.

And thinking to himself, *But if they're real, God help us all.*

THE PYRAMID HOTEL

Gideon Thorn returned from walking Angelina to her boarding house, his mind awhirl with thoughts. The lady was attractive, certainly, but she was also *nosy,* a prerequisite for journalistic triumph. While attracted to her, Thorn knew she would never cease prying, however gently, sympathetically, until she'd learned every last detail of his past, some parts of which he chose to keep private.

Besides, what did it matter how she looked, or even if she liked him in some way beyond the bounds of her profession? Thorn had set himself a task—a mission—that did not include entanglements with women on the road. A brief liaison on occasion, strictly cash and carry, was permissible. A love affair, ensnaring hearts and minds, was not.

Thorn stripped, washed in the room's ceramic basin, and examined, as he often did, the mirror image of his pendants dangling from a silver chain around his neck. They were religious symbols, clumped together without primacy given to any one of them: a cross, a pentagram, a crescent, and a Star of David, representing Christianity, Wicca, Islam and Judaism. So far he had failed to locate symbols relevant to Buddhism or Hinduism, but he hoped to find them someday in his travels.

Meanwhile, he had dragons on his mind.

He'd left the lady editor with food for thought, enough to profile him for readers of *The Hieroglyph,* but nothing that should hinder him. If anyone came forward with a dragon sighting or some unrelated story of their own, so much the better. And if not, he'd be no worse off than before. Perhaps New Egypt's townspeople would see him in a better light—or, just as probably, some might well shy away from him.

No matter.

Thorn had already decided on his next step. If the creature, whatever it was, had been unearthed eight days ago—now almost nine—it had to eat. He couldn't see it waiting eight days for its first feeding, on Chan Li Gong, particularly if it were as large as witnesses maintained. To Thorn, that meant it had been eating somewhere else in the meantime, gathering strength and confidence before its first raid on Celestial Alley.

First thing in the morning, after breakfast, he would talk to Marshal Rockwell about local ranchers missing any of their stock. Thorn hoped the lawman wouldn't still be smoldering over their chance encounter on the street, with Angelina Farnum, but he couldn't let that slow him down. Thorn's first priority was to identify the creature, then determine how to deal with it. Smoothing the marshal's ruffled feathers didn't enter into it. No private feelings, much less fretting over someone else's tender toes, was going to divert Thorn from his quest.

With that in mind, he lay down on the bed, his gunbelt looped over the brass post nearest his right hand. His Sharps was in the chifforobe, but Thorn's Winchester shared the mattress with him, close against his side. If someone tried to force the door's lock and the chair he'd wedged beneath its knob, the racket would alert him, giving Thorn sufficient time to mount a stiff defense.

Unlikely, but precautions were designed to ward off trouble, not to compensate for it.

He had been nearing drowsy when he pushed back from the table in the hotel's restaurant, but walking Angelina home and bumping into Marshal Rockwell on the street had cleared the cobwebs from Thorn's mind. While he was coming back alone, he'd tried to picture Angelina and the lawman as a couple, but they didn't fit. Not that he was an expert in that field, by any means, but Thorn had sensed that Rockwell wanted more from their relationship, whatever that might be, than Angelina was prepared to offer him.

Just friends. The saddest words a yearning heart could ever here, or so Thorn had been told.

Did that make Seth an adversary or a threat? Thorn hoped not, but he couldn't delve into the marshal's mind and, even if he could, would not have cared to try.

Holding that thought in mind, he drifted off to sleep.

George Hearst was dozing lightly, dreaming of a gold vein eight to ten feet wide, running the full length of a shaft that wound for miles into the earth. The claim was his, and it would multiply his fortune ten- or twentyfold, at least. He was ecstatic, ready to attack the gleaming treasure with his pick—when suddenly, a rapid beating on his door jarred him from sleep and made him bolt upright in bed.

"The hell is that?" he shouted, wanting his displeasure to be obvious.

"It's Clete, sir. Gotta see you right away."

"Just hold your water," Hearst commanded, rolling out of bed and reaching for his trousers folded on a nearby chair. No matter what the crisis, he refused to meet subordinates in his long underwear alone.

Barefoot, still groggy, he moved to the door and opened it, admitting Alford with his hat in hand. "All right," Hearst said. "What's all the racket leading up to?"

"Trouble at the Silver Crown, sir. Otis sent me in to tell you."

"Spit it out, then."

"Um, I ain't sure how to say it, Mr.—"

"Open up your trap and string the words together, just like anybody else."

"But this is *bad* news."

"If you say that one more time without explaining, I may have to knock you down."

"Yes, sir. Somethin' attacked the mine tonight, beat down some of the boys and got the Cornish all riled up."

"Some*thing*?"

"Yes, sir. It carried off Jed Tabor."

"One of yours? The agency's?"

"Yes, sir. Snatched 'im right off his feet and flew away with 'im, just like a hawk grabbin' a mouse."

Hearst felt the short hairs on his nape bristling. He glared at Alford, walked across the sitting room and came back to his starting point, still staring holes into the Pinkerton. "That sounds like a demented fantasy," he said.

"I wish it was, Boss."

"Let me smell your breath."

Hearst leaned in close and Alford heaved a sigh into his face. His teeth could use a cleaning, but there was no reek of alcohol.

Confirming it, Clete said, "I ain't drunk, Mr. Hearst. Neither was Otis nor the rest."

"How many of you saw this flying thing?"

"Can't say, exactly. There was Otis, all my boys on night shift—which is twelve—and half as many Cornishmen outside the shaft, dumping their ore and backfill, others workin' on the stamp mills."

"So you'd say about two dozen, then?"

"Easy. Yes, sir."

"And you fired on it?"

"Me and the other boys. Jed had his six-gun out and blastin' when it snatched him up. It didn't seem to feel a thing."

"And Mr. Breen sent you to tell me."

"Right, sir."

Now Hearst felt as if he'd swallowed down a lump of lead, in place of Aunt Lou's chicken with the fixings. Careful not to show it, he advised the Pinkerton, "There's nothing to be done about it now, tonight. I'll be out first thing in the morning, maybe with the marshal, maybe not."

Thinking before he finished saying it, *Fat lot of good that bumpkin is.*

"We'll need more men," he said. "That's certain. Find another fellow you can spare and send him to Fort Davis at first light. Another message for Chicago, telling them I want to double up their force around the Silver Crown."

"Yes, sir. You want me to, I'll carry it myself."

He seemed too eager. Hearst squashed that, telling him, "No, Clete. You're my second in command. Send someone junior, bottom of the ladder."

"Yes, sir. I already got someone in mind."

"The main thing, now, is making sure the Cornish keep their noses to the grindstone. Work goes on, no matter what. They fear what's in the air, it should encourage them to work hard underground."

"There's been some talk of walking out. I won't deny it, sir."

"Step hard on that," said Hearst. "A man who quits on me is finished in the mining industry. Word gets around, he won't be hired in any mine or factory from Frisco back to Philadelphia. And once he's on the blacklist, with his family, they *stay* there till they starve or run for home. Be crystal-clear on that."

"Yes, sir."

"Make sure they understand I'm deadly serious."

"No problem, sir."

"And Clete?"

"Yes, sir?" The Pinkerton stopped where he was, hand on the doorknob.

"If you see any kind of monster flying by, do everything

within your power to bring it down. We need to stop this shit posthaste."

TEN

NEW EGYPT: JULY 15, 1875

Thorn was the first one down for breakfast at The Pyramid, already looking forward to Aunt Lou's next offering. This morning's special was a sirloin steak with two fried eggs, shredded potatoes also fried until they were a golden brown, and grilled tomatoes on the side., with black coffee to top it off.

His meal arrived, and as he worked his way around the plate, savoring each flavor in turn, Thorn watched the restaurant fill up. Some guests he recognized and others whom he didn't came downstairs, while customers with no rooms at The Pyramid came off the thoroughfare. None made a point of staring at him, but Thorn felt their eyes flicking across the room toward him, and then away, when they believed he would not notice them.

A part of that was what he called the "stranger syndrome," people's natural reaction to an unfamiliar person in their midst. The rest—most of it, he surmised— came from New Egypt's gossip mill, word circulating of his mission, changing and misstating it along the way, until he turned into an even greater curiosity than fact alone would justify. If Thorn had been alone, it might have made him smile, but pinioned in the public eye, he kept his face deadpan and gave them nothing back.

As he ate his meal, gazing around the room, faces half-turned in his direction jerked back toward their own plates and companions, people who would call themselves respectable caught spying on another like small children with a new kid in a schoolroom. That made Thorn inclined to take his time, stretch out his breakfast, tantalizing them with mysteries conjured by their imaginations.

Thorn was some three-quarters done when Angelina Farnum came into the restaurant, saw him, and made directly for his table. She wore blue satin, with crinoline beneath the bell-shaped skirt to fill it out, her matching shoes just visible below the hem. A lighter bonnet, perched atop her head, had shielded her from sun outside, and now she left it on as she approached his table.

Sitting uninvited, she asked Thorn, "What have you heard about last night?"

"Last night?" he answered back, confused.

"So, nothing, then?"

"Is this a riddle?"

Leaning forward, lowering her voice, she said, "Some *thing* dropped half a man over Celestial Alley."

"Half?"

"Suspicion is that it's one of the Pinkertons snatched from the Silver Crown."

Thorn set his knife and fork down quietly. "Explain."

"The dragon, creature, whatever you call it, paid a call on Hearst's people last night. They fired some shots, it knocked some people down, and then made off with one of them, a Jed Tabor, one of Hearst's guards. Unless it grabbed somebody else along its way back to New Egypt, he's the one—his lower half, at least—that dropped into Celestial Alley."

"And you heard all this from...?"

"Seth Rockwell. He rode out to the Silver Crown at dawn and talked to Hearst, some of the others. There were witnesses, at least a couple dozen of them, and they all agree that something huge and terrifying *flew* into the camp and started raising hell."

"Sorry I missed it," Thorn admitted, picking up his fork again and going for another bite of steak.

"That's why I'm here," she said.

"What is?"

"To see if you want in."

"We're back to riddles now. In *what?*"

"The Powers That Be are meeting at the undertaker's parlor, straight up seven. I'm among them, thankfully, as leader of the local fourth estate. You want to come along?"

"As what?" Thorn asked.

"My hired investigator," Angelina answered.

"When did you hire me?"

"Right now, if you're agreeable."

Thorn checked his pocket watch and saw they had just ten minutes to spare before the gathering began. He put his money on the table, speared a final bite of steak and egg, chewing it as he rose and put his hat on.

"One thing," Angelina said. "Be quiet as a church mouse when we get there. Let me do the talking—for the newspaper, you understand?"

"I'll do my best," Thorn said, and hoped that he could manage it.

The undertaker's mortuary, two blocks north, stood next to a physician's office, which Thorn personally thought was awkward placement for the latter, freighted with dire possibilities. They entered, Thorn holding the door for Angelina, heralded by a small bell above the door, and followed muffled voices to a room in back.

Four men were there ahead of them, all pausing in the middle of their conversation, faces swiveling to greet the new arrivals with expressions ranging from mild curiosity to thinly veiled anger. The anger came from Seth Rockwell, the only other person present whom Thorn recognized.

"Gentlemen," said Angelina, "sorry if we kept you waiting, though I do believe it's just 6:59."

"And what's he doing here?" the marshal asked, barely disguising his hostility.

"I have retained him as my personal investigator for *The Hieroglyph,* now that we have two incidents and both are unexplained." Facing the others in their turn, from left to right beyond the lawman, Angelina said, "Gideon Thorn, meet Ethan Neagle, mayor of New Egypt. Next to him is Dr. Millard Gilmore, our physician, and behind the table is Isaiah Kent, our undertaker."

Thorn nodded at each of them in turn, no shaking hands under the circumstances, and received a range of muttered greetings, mostly curious, in turn. The six of them now formed a circle around what Thorn took for Kent's embalming table, occupied at present by a partial corpse under a bloodstained sheet. The feet protruding from one end told Thorn the body had been truncated somewhere around mid-chest, taking the head, shoulders and arms away.

"Can we see him now?" asked Angelina. "What there is of him?"

The undertaker glanced at Rockwell and received a nod before he drew the sheet back. Someone had undressed the body and it lay supine, a ragged wound extending from one armpit to the other, more or less across the upper part of what had been a well-muscled and hairy chest. From that huge wound protruded veins, muscles and tendons, parts of the thoracic organs. Down below, the legs were crushed and twisted, likely from the drop into Celestial Alley.

"Well," the marshal said, "at least we know the cause of death."

"Do we?" asked Angelina with a biting tone approaching sarcasm. "Can you describe what happened here, Marshal? Was this man *sawed* apart, or was the upper portion of his body *ripped* off. And in either case, by what or whom?"

Turning a fuchsia color from his collar up, Rockwell began to say, "I only meant—"

The doctor cut him off, saying, "Neither, in fact. As Mr. Kent and I agree, this is a bite wound."

"What in holy—" Mayor Neagle remembered that they had a lady present and rephrased his question. "What exactly are you saying, Doc? That somethin' *chewed* this fella's head and all right off the top of 'im?"

"I said a bite wound, not a gnawing wound," Gilmore replied, "but it amounts to the same thing. And yes, that's what we're saying."

"You agree with that, Isaiah?" Neagle asked.

The undertaker nodded. "Yes, regrettably."

"And how long would that take?" asked Angelina.

Dr. Gilmore swallowed, said, "We estimate a bite or

two, no more than three, together with some tugging at the end."

"But that would mean... It must be huge," she said.

"Undoubtedly," the doctor said, Kent nodding in agreement.

"Not a bear or cougar, then," said Angelina.

"Many times the size of either one," Gilmore replied. "And no pack of coyotes, either, before somebody suggests it."

"All right," Rockwell interjected, sounding almost numb. "So, what could do something like that?"

"That I'm aware of, possibly one of the larger sharks at sea," said Gilmore, "but we're obviously landlocked. Or a giant crocodile from Africa or Asia, but again..." He let the observation trail off, incomplete.

"Now that we're done with fantasy," Mayor Neagle said, "what did it that might live around these parts?"

"Nothing I ever saw before," said Gilmore. Kent nodded again on that score.

"Something that we've *heard* of, though," said Angelina giving voice to what they'd all been thinking silently.

"Don't start that dragon crap again," said Rockwell.

"All right. What do *you* suggest, Marshal?" she challenged him. When he did not respond, she forged ahead. "At least two dozen people saw one of the Pinkertons snatched up from Hearst's claim, carried off into the night. The word's all over town. A short time later, *this* drops from the sky into Celestial Alley. Are you claiming that's *coincidence?*"

"I wish to hell I know," Rockwell said, dully. "I already talked to Hearst, his foremen, and some others at the Silver Crown today. They stand together, sayin' it's some kinda trick put on by 'enemies,' implyin' Randolph Boone could be behind it. Never mind he's goin' out of business as we stand here, from his miners runnin' off."

"And so, we're back to *what*," said Angelina, this time staring hard at each of them in turn. "Suggestions? Anyone?"

When no one spoke after a long, slow minute, she said, "Come on, Mr. Thorne. I'd say we need to find a dragon."

Thus far, Thorn had kept his promise to keep quiet, but he paused as they approached the exit, turning back to Rockwell. "Marshal, may I ask if any farmers in the area have mentioned missing stock within the past nine days?"

Rockwell stared at him as if Thorn had grown a second head. At last, he said, "Nobody's said nothin' to me. You wanna run around and ask 'em all, feel free."

SILVER CROWN MINE

The rider from Fort Davis came in tired and sweating through his clothes, his lemonsilla gelding lathered after galloping from town out to the mine. George Hearst was questioning his manager when he saw Otis Breen glance up and followed Breen's eyes to the horseman reining in.

Clete Alford got there just ahead of Hearst, was starting to interrogate the rider when he saw Hearst bearing down on him and shifted from a question to an introduction. "Mr. Hearst, Alton Coleman."

Coleman doffed his hat and bobbed his head toward Hearst. "G'day, sir."

"Well," Hearst said, "what news of Mr. Thorn?"

The rider's throat was croaking dry, so Hearst allowed him just the smallest sip of canteen water first, before he spilled his news. That done, Coleman asked Hearst, "You want it any special way, sir?"

"Did you get it down in writing, or am I trusting your memory?" Hearst countered.

"Written, sir. And lengthy, too."

"I'll take that, then," Hearst said, extending his right hand.

Coleman withdrew a long, white envelope from somewhere on the inside of his dusty jacket, passing it to Hearst. The mining baron hefted it, frowned at its weight, and told the messenger, "Go on and get some rest, now. I'll send for you if there's anything unclear to me."

"Yes, sir. Thank you."

While Coleman led his horse away, Hearst turned to Breen and said, "Inside," immediately making for the manager's small hut and office. Breen was on his heels, Clete Alford trailing, asking one or both of them, "Should I come, too?"

"No need," Hearst said, dismissing him, and clomped into Breen's temporary home ahead of him, dropping behind the desk and leaving Breen the only other chair, a straight-backed wooden thing of little comfort.

Opening the envelope, Hearst pulled four sheets of yellow paper with the information he'd requested from Chicago printed out by hand in square block capitals. He skimmed the contents, then went back and started at the top, reading in detail while Breen studied blunt hands folded in his lap. From time to time, Hearst called out points of interest to his manager.

"Our boy's just twenty-three years old," Hearst said. "Orphaned at two, an animal attack at home, along the Colorado Rockies. Soon retrieved by his last living relative, an aunt in Boston—and, oho, she's rich! Well, *he* is, now, since she passed on the summer after Mr. Thorn left Harvard with a *summa cum laude* and plans for law school. All kinds of sports teams in addition to his normal classes, blah-blah-blah. Decided *not* to study law in lieu of traveling, researching incidents that he considers mysteries, perhaps shedding some light upon his private tragedy."

"What brings him here, then?" Breen inquired. "His folks killed by a flying monster?"

"No suggestion of it," Hearst replied. "My guess would be obsession. It takes hold, you know."

Breen nodded, eyes downcast at that, and kept his mouth shut tight.

"It seems that Mr. Thorn's only remaining contact in the East, aside from lawyers and accountants, is a nigger servant of his aunt's—well, African, in fact, brought over as a youngster prior to Emancipation. Seems to be eccentric in his own right. Name's Obi Magoro. Where do they come up with monikers like that, Otis?"

"Tribal, I'd guess," the manager replied.

"No doubt. The upshot being that our Mr. Thorn is not simply another saddle bum with loose bees in his bonnet. Money on his scale can be a force to reckon with."

"Yes, sir."

Folding the pages back into their envelope and stowing it away, Hearst said, "I'll have to give this youngster some more thought."

THE HIEROGLYPH'S OFFICE

"What about those ranchers?"

"It was just a passing question," Thorn told Angelina.

They were seated at her desk, her notes and steaming coffee mugs between them.

"Oh, I got the reference," she said. "Stock missing, and a monster needs to eat. I'm asking if you'll go around and question them."

"Haven't decided yet. Was Rockwell lying, do you think, when he denied any reports of disappearances?"

"I'd normally say 'no,' but since he seems to have a grudge against you..."

"You're the grudge," Thorn said, and watched her blush a little, reaching for her coffee.

"Well, I can't help that," she said.

"Maybe if you just let him down."

"What makes you think I haven't?" she replied, defensively.

Thorn raised his hands in mock surrender. "Not my business. Sorry."

"No, it isn't." Softening, she said, "As to this monster, it's a man-eater?"

"One missing, one chewed up, in two days' time. Seems like it, but we don't know what it lived on, down there in the mine, however long that was."

"What do you know about suspended animation?" she inquired.

"Akin to hibernation, but conceivably of much longer duration based on scientific theory. Slowing or stoppage of the life processes by exogenous or endogenous means without termination. Breathing, heartbeat, and other involuntary functions may still occur, but they can only be detected by external, artificial means."

She blinked at him. "That sounds like something quoted from a textbook."

"Probably." Thorn tapped his temple with an index finger. "Photographic memory."

"That's handy."

"Sometimes," he agreed. "At others, I'd be happy to forget."

"Your family?"

"We've covered that, I think," he answered, rather stiffly.

"Not for publication," she assured him. "I was just...well, curious."

"All right. For purposes of private conversation only, I remember them by choice. They keep me searching. Other things, like Bledsoe's Home for Orphaned Boys and things that happened coming up through school, I could get by without."

"They made you who and what you are today, though," Angelina said.

He smiled. "Whatever *that* is?"

"An investigator. Someone who solves riddles."

"Tries to, anyway. Speaking of which..."

"Our dragon."

"Right. Suppose—and this is just a theory I've been working on—suppose it's something prehistoric that's survived somehow, into the modern era?"

"Like a dinosaur, you mean?"

Thorn knew that a British scientist, one Richard Owen, had proposed the ancient existence of the *Dinosauria*, combining the Greek words for "terrible" and "lizard," back in 1841, after extensive study of fossils deposited long eons before mankind clambered down from trees or crawled out of the caves. Owen's work—like that of Charles Darwin, author of *The Origin of Species*—remained controversial, particularly among die-hard Biblical literalists.

"That's exactly right!" she said, enthused now. "What if one of them was trapped below ground, somehow, and slipped into this suspended animation while time passed it by? What if the miners woke it and released it on the world again?"

"A creature out of place and time," Thorn said. "It's possible in theory, but you know it must have been confined a long, *long* time. No sustenance we know of, maybe just a little air."

"I'll leave that problem to the scientists, assuming that it's ever caught or killed. And if I'm wrong...well, I'm just theorizing, anyway."

"As good as any, I suppose."

"And were there any *flying* dinosaurs?"

"Apparently, there were," Thorn said, "though strictly speaking, they're called pterosaurs, Latin for 'wing lizards.' Italian naturalist Cosimo Collini found the first fossils in 1741 but misinterpreted their wings as paddles. Georges Cuvier of France turned that around in 1801 and named the genus *Pterodactylus* eight years later. Others expanded that into the family *Pterosauria* in 1862."

Angelina fairly gaped at him. "Good, Lord, Thorn! Is there anything you *don't* know?"

"Plenty," he replied, smiling. "Including anything I haven't seen or read."

"And where would we go looking for a pterodactyl in the Lone Star State today?"

He lost the smile and said, "Someplace where it can hide by daylight, or we'd have reports arriving daily, maybe hourly. But you're the local. Any thoughts?"

Angelina pondered that, then said, "I might, at that."

ELEVEN

BOOT HILL, NEW EGYPT

Gideon joined Angelina Farnum for the funeral. He could have passed, but it was too late in the afternoon to start a tour of surrounding ranches, and if he was going to continue posing as the publisher's investigator, Thorn supposed that he should act like it.

Besides, he'd found that he enjoyed her company.

The guest of honor at the planting was the mutilated body found in Celestial Alley. George Hearst, in attendance with a couple of his Pinkertons, confirmed the dead man's name—Jed Tabor—and his late position with the Eye That Never Sleeps as one of its "industrial detectives." Hearst had made arrangements with Chicago for the burial in Texas, he proclaimed, to spare the victim's family from any further trauma caused by viewing his remains.

"Do you believe that story?" Angelina whispered to him, standing near graveside, among eleven dry-eyed mourners.

"I believe he was a Pinkerton, all right," Thorn said.

"The rest of it?"

He shrugged.

New Egypt had no church, leaving Isaiah Kent, the undertaker, to preside over the funeral. He said something about a young man cut down in his prime, although they had no clue regarding Tabor's age, then spoke about the terror in their midst and quoted from Isaiah chapter 27 without opening the Bible in his hand.

"In that day," Kent proclaimed, "the Lord with his sore and great and strong sword shall punish leviathan the piercing serpent, even leviathan that crooked serpent; and he shall slay the dragon that is in the sea. Amen!"

"Which doesn't help us much with serpents in the air," said Angelina, *sotto voce,* almost causing Thorn to laugh aloud. He swallowed it instead and kept a straight face as George Hearst, then his two armed companions, took turns with a spade, dropping raw earth atop Jed Tabor's plain pine box.

Angelina jotted observations on her pad, Thorn noting that she wrote in shorthand to condense the text. "Would you call that a moving service?" she asked.

"Pretty standard, if you cut out God killing the sea serpent."

"No one here who knew the victim except Hearst and his two gunmen."

"That we know of."

As he spoke, Thorn cut a glance toward Marshal Rockwell, standing well apart, ten paces from the spectators who were dispersing now, frowning at Hearst, his hirelings, and the open grave.

"Oh, Gideon," she said. "You don't think Seth would strike a bargain with—"

"The richest man he'll likely ever meet? It never crossed my mind," he said.

"You're cynical."

"Or realistic, as the case may be."

"What would he gain from that?" she pressed him.

"Money, possibly the promise of a staff job somewhere down the line, when Hearst moves on. Hearst, for his dollar, would obtain an inside view of anything reported to the marshal's office, anything the law dug up about his rivals or whatever else he's interested in, from local politics and gossip to the county level."

"No," said Angelina, with a stern shake of her head. "I don't believe that."

"Fair enough. He's your friend," Thorn replied. "I barely know him."

"And you care for him no more than he does you."

"I'm funny that way. When somebody hates me, I don't feel all warm and friendly toward him."

"I don't think he *hates,* you."

"Close enough for lawman's work," Thorn said, casting a final look toward Rockwell as the marshal turned away and started walking back to town.

A pair of hired gravediggers went to work on Tabor's hole, filling it in swiftly, ignoring those who'd turned out for the service. Thorn saw Hearst slip greenbacks into Kaiser's hand, payment for burying his man and reading over him. The undertaker nodded, pocketed the cash, and stayed to watch the spade men finish their appointed task.

"Do you suppose he'll have a marker, Gideon?"

"It's probably included in the price."

"I wish I had a camera," she said. "Before much longer, they'll be all the rage with newspapers."

They turned away, faced back toward town, some sixty yards due west, and had advanced only a few steps when a gruff, familiar voice called out behind them, "Mr. Thorn! A word, if you don't mind?"

Thorn stopped and turned, saw Hearst advancing on him from the grave, his gunmen flanking him and hanging back a stride or two behind their boss. Hearst had a handkerchief in his left hand and dabbed his forehead with it, blotting sweat, before he tucked it out of sight inside his tweed jacket.

"What do you want?" Thorn asked, keepin a civil tone but nothing more.

"I've just been reading up on you," Hearst said.

"Another hobby?"

"Let's just say I make a point of studying potential adversaries."

"You've mistaken me for someone else," Thorn said.

"The nephew of Drusilla Thorn, old Boston money rooted in the shipping industry, whaling, and other enterprises? Did my inquiries settle upon the wrong Gideon Thorn, by some peculiar twist of circumstance?"

"They're accurate so far," Gideon said.

"Thorn money," Hearst replied. "*Serious* money. Makes me wonder if you might be moving inland, as it were, to sink some of that loot in mining claims."

"Then you can rest in peace." Thorn could feel Angelina watching him, and caught an image from the corner of his eye: her pencil moving, scribbling shorthand notes.

"I seldom rest," Hearst said, "and even then uneasily."

"Sounds like a problem for a doctor."

"It's eternal vigilance, in fact. To build and *hold* an empire, you must have it covered, all at once. Think of a spider web. Each time an insect plucks one of the strands, its builder moves to face the threat or claim a meal."

"And sucks them dry," Thorn said.

"Survival of the fittest," Hearst replied. "Now you arrive, from nowhere as it were—"

"From Tularosa, in New Mexico," said Thorn correcting him.

"—and what should happen, but a *dragon* suddenly emerges from a mine I hoped to purchase, driving off its brainless heathen workers, while a rich vein waits below."

"And how would you know that?" asked Angelina, pencil poised.

Ignoring her, Hearst told Thorn, "Do you call that mere coincidence?"

"I call it poor chronology," Gideon said. "This creature first appeared while I was in New Mexico."

"*You* say!"

"And since you can't prove otherwise—or even if you think you can—that's no concern of yours. I don't answer to you. I have no interest in your 'empire,' save where it impedes the progress of my own investigation."

"For the local newspaper," Hearst fairly sneered.

"And on my own behalf. No business of yours, in any case."

Hearst bristled. "*I* decide what is or is not my concern, my business."

"Until you set your sights on butting into mine."

"Do you flatly deny a plan to buy the Silver Belle?"

Thorn saw the chink in Hearst's armor—or one of them, at least. It wasn't large, just simple insecurity, but that could drive him to excess, unbalance him, and what might happen then?

"We're done here," Thorn replied, a near-smile playing on his face.

Hearst reddened, snarling as Thorn turned away, "*I* am not done with *you*." Three paces later, he called out, "I hope that nothing happens to your nigger, back in Boston."

Thorn stopped dead, turned on his heel, and strode back into Heart's personal space, their chests almost touching. He saw the *pistoleros* fidgeting on either side of Hearst and kept his own hands clamped onto his twin Colt Peacemakers.

"Obi Magoro is a better man than you in all respects," he told the mining king. "I have no doubt that he could mop the floor with you and any dozen of your hired assassins on the worst day of his life. But just in case your arrogance propels you toward some foolishness that cannot be undone, know this: if *anything* happens to him—a streetcar accident, a mugging, or a bolt of lightning from the blue— I'm holding *you* responsible. And you're an easy man to find."

"Threats, now?" Hearst answered, with an unfamiliar quaver in his voice.

"A promise you can bank on, George."

Again, Thorn turned away, and this time Hearst was silent as he left the graveyard, Angelina at his side. Thorn felt the rich man staring after him, eyes boring into Thorn's back like twin gun barrels, but nothing short of gunfire from behind would make him turn and face the older man again.

"I can't believe you talked to him like that," said Angelina.

"Someone ought to do it every day, so he remembers that he's not the Lord of all creation."

"Are you sure about that?" she inquired.

Returning to New Egypt proper, even though most of the shops were closing for the day, they found a fair number of residents at large and stirring on the thoroughfare. It only took a moment to pick out an orator who was addressing the townsfolk, black-clad like Gideon, but with a stiff white collar turned around to indicate he was some kind of clergyman.

"Someone you recognize?" Thorn asked.

"I've never seen him in my life," said Angelina.

And no church in town, Gideon told himself. The backwards collar could belong to any one of nine or ten diverse and often mutually hostile Christian sects, which told him nothing. Moving closer, Angelina at his side, he saw the man was standing on an upturned crate to raise himself about his clustered audience, no Bible in his hands, both gesturing to punctuate his words.

"My friends!" he told the crowd, all strangers to him if he was a new arrival in the settlement, "you have a problem in New Egypt and its name is *heathenism.*"

No one rose to it immediately, but a few of the onlookers muttered back and forth, while Angelina glanced at Thorn and asked him, "What on Earth?"

"See where he goes with this," Thorn said.

"I travel far and wide combating Satan!" said the orator. "Each settlement I visit, he is there before me, always in a different guise. Sometimes he's gambling, selling rotgut, smoking opium, or peddling shameless women. Rarely is it that I find the whole lot rolled up into one, but when I do, it always spells *celestials!*"

The crowd was growing, and its murmuring picked up in volume.

"Here, you've had a white man murdered—one you're *sure* of—and his body savaged. Who claims they 'discovered' it? *Celestials*. And where? The alley where they congregate, offering vices to whichever sinners have the cash on hand. You have a paying mine outside of town, shut down because *celestials* and *Mexicans* insist they saw a dragon slither out of it and fly away. Imagine all the silver that will never find its way into your coffers, will not feed your families, while heathens spread their tales of giant lizards on the wing. And who worships the dragon in their far off land of opium and incense? *The celestials!*"

A growl rose from the crowd now, which had roughly doubled around Thorn and Angelina. On his crate, the speaker flashed a set of yellow teeth and shook his fist skyward, as if inviting thunderbolts.

"How long must Lord Jehovah in his heaven suffer such a travesty?" he cried. "How long must *you* put up with vipers nesting in the heart of your community, obstructing progress, undermining morals and the raw vitality of native sons and daughters? How long will it be until you find yourselves polluted and debased into a *mongrel* race of beings no longer familiar with the image of their God?"

"There's Seth," said Angelina, moving toward the marshal where he stood, off to the far left of the crowd. Thorn trailed her, wondering what she would say to Rockwell, what she hoped he might achieve.

Reaching the lawman, Angelina asked him, "Do you know this fellow, Seth?"

"He's new to me," the marshal answered, eyes still on the orator.

"What do you plan to do about him?"

"Do?" Now Rockwell peered at her, looking confused.

"He's standing there, inciting your neighbors to riot!" Angelina said.

Seth frowned. "I'd call it free speech, Mrs. Farnum. You can find it in the First Amendment, right beside your freedom of the press."

"You'd simply let him go ahead, then?"

"As opposed to gagging him?" asked Rockwell. "Maybe tossing him in jail?"

"Inciting riots is a felony."

"And near impossible to prove, at least without a *riot*. Now, if that happens, me and my deputies will take all necessary steps required to put a lid on it and keep the town in working order."

"Afterward," she said, glaring at Seth.

"That's how the law works, ma'am. We don't lock people up because they *might* commit a crime someday."

"If this ends badly, Marshal, you'll be featured on *The Hieroglyph*'s front page."

"Save me a copy, Mrs. Farnum. Now, if you don't mind, I'm going on patrol."

THE PYRAMID

"Two dinners in two nights. What will the gossips say?"

Thorn turned from Angelina, looked around the restaurant, and found its normal crown reduced by some three-fourths. He spotted Randolph Boone and nodded to the mining boss, then swiveled back.

"It looks like most of them are missing it," he said. "Between the dragon and that shouter on the street, they're otherwise engaged."

"About him," Angelina said. "Doesn't it strike you as peculiar, turning up in New Egypt right now, with all that's going on?"

"Peculiar doesn't cover it."

"So, *why?*"

"One thought I had," Thorn said, "connects him back to Hearst. Don't quote me on it, but..."

"Go on."

"I haven't been here long and didn't recognize his face, but if you take the collar off and put a gunbelt on him, he could be one of the Pinkertons guarding the Silver Crown."

Angelina sliced into her breaded pork chop with a vengeance. "Say you're right. What would he gain from stirring up a riot? Hearst, I mean."

"Well, if he's thinking someone might eliminate the dragon, monster, whatever it is, and Boone might get his miners back, eliminating half of them would slow the Belle Aire's operation down."

Thorn ate part of his chop with mashed potatoes and a kind of chicken gravy while she thought about it, scowling back at him from her side of the table. "That's outrageous!"

"It was just a thought."

"I mean that *Hearst* would think of it."

"Remember what I said. I'm only speculating, throwing out ideas. I could be wrong."

"But if you're *right*, if Seth is on his payroll—"

"Now—"

"—that would explain why he just shrugged the preacher off and let him spread his poison."

"On the other hand, there *is* the First Amendment. People say all kinds of stupid things in public every day, no end of them in Congress, when you think about it."

"I don't live in Congress," Angelina told him. "I live

here. And if some bully out of San Francisco or Nevada thinks he can waltz in here like a foreign potentate and throw his weight around, his money, why... I don't know what I'd do!"

"Report it in your newspaper?"

"That's right!"

"But first, you need the facts," he cautiously reminded her. "Hearst has money to burn on libel suits that might bankrupt you, even if you win. Or he could go another route and start a paper of his own, steal advertisers, undersell you, run you out of business."

"One more reason why I hate him!" Setting down her fork, she told Thorn, "Now I've lost my appetite."

"Think twice about that," Thorn replied. "You need your strength for the campaign."

She nodded, raised the fork again. "And even if his bogus 'aunt' *did* cook it, this is good!"

When their plates were nearly clean, she asked him, "How would you find out about the preacher?"

"Likely check on where he's staying," Thorn replied. "If he's not sleeping at The Pyramid, what does that leave?"

"New Egypt has two boarding houses, and he's not at mine."

"That only leaves one possibility, or..."

Angelina got it. "He could go back to the Silver Crown and bed down with the other Pinkertons."

"No easy way to check on that tonight," said Gideon.

"And if there's trouble, I should be here."

"But in the morning, if the town's still standing, I—or we—could ride out there and have a look around."

"Discreetly."

"Right. Like spies." She smiled. "What time should that be?"

"If we make it through the night? I'd say first thing, right after breakfast."

"I dine at the boarding house," she said.

"And I can meet you at the livery. You ride?"

"Of course!"

"Because a trap would be—"

"Too slow and cumbersome."

"Exactly. What about dessert?"

"Peach cobbler," she remembered from the menu. "It would be a shame to pass on that."

"Right. Two it is, then."

Thorn was looking forward to tomorrow, the adventure of it, and the fact of spending more time in the lady's company. Whatever happened that night, or tomorrow morning, he had cast the gauntlet down for Hearst and was intrigued to see the man's next move.

TWELVE

THE PYRAMID

"Have you stirred them up enough?" George Hearst demanded. "In your personal opinion as an agitator?"

"Yes, sir," Raynard Dunn replied, glancing around at the appointments of Hearst's suite and finding that they didn't live up to his expectations for a rich man.

"And you'll be on hand to stoke the fire, once it gets going?"

"Absolutely, sir."

Dunn wore the suit and backwards collar he'd been sporting on the thoroughfare, an hour earlier. He'd come into The Pyramid via the back way, under orders to avoid crossing the lobby, a precaution that he recognized of old. As a *provocateur* and agitator for the Pinkertons, he'd riled up striking miners, anarchists and communists, Irish members of the Fenians and Clan na Gael, for whom he'd practiced and perfected a convincing brogue. On one occasion, when it seemed that jurors might acquit a gang of railroad bandits apprehended by his fellow Pinkertons, he'd even led a lynch mob that dispensed rough justice without recourse to a jury's vote.

"All right, Raynard," Hearst said, drawing a roll of greenback from his trouser pocket. "Here's the first five hundred that we talked about. You get the other five when I receive word that Celestial Alley is no more."

"As good as done, sir."

At the final instant, as his fingers gripped the money, Hearst hung onto it. "But Raynard, listen to me closely."

"Yes, sir."

"If the Chinks are still around come sunup, and their hovels standing, I expect a full refund."

"Of course, sir. Absolutely! If you'd rather hold the money until then—"

"No, no. A deal's a deal."

"Yes, sir. And thank you. What about the Mexicans?"

"They're being taken care of," Hearts replied. "Your brethren of the Eye That Never Sleeps will deal with them tonight, as well, while residents of this fine sty are busy mopping up the Yellow Peril."

"Ah. Yes, sir." Dunn couldn't help admiring how the old man's mind worked, taking problems as they came, knocking them down, with nothing left to chance. He knew that's how a man got rich and stayed rich, wondering why he had never managed it himself.

"Before you go to light the final fuse," Hearst told him, "take some time off for yourself. Have dinner. Not downstairs, of course. That wouldn't do. Perhaps the Mother Lode? I understand they make a tolerable stew." The old man cracked a smile, adding, "I doubt you'd care for Chinese food."

"No, sir." Dunn happily returned the smile, a sign of favor from the man in charge of this assignment.

As he turned to leave, Hearst spoke again, stopping him at the door. "Tonight," the old man said, "when things get rolling, even if you feel a mighty motivation, I would urge you in the strongest terms to shed no yellow blood yourself."

"Sir?"

"Keep in mind who you're supposed to be, and who you represent. Your usefulness continues only while you have a certain reputation, albeit created out of whole cloth, for behaving in a certain way. You're an *exhorter,* Raynard, but you would not stoop to soil your hands when there are other audiences to electrify, passions to rouse. Why waste your precious time in prison, or procure an invitation to an air dance?"

Thinking of the gallows made Dunn blanch a little, swallowing to make sure that his windpipe wasn't being crushed.

"No, sir. I understand."

"Good man. I'll see you in the morning, at the Silver Crown."

"Stay here," said Angelina, as they stood outside The Pyramid. "I know my way back to the boarding house."

"No, ma'am. A gentleman always escorts a lady home."

She half-smiled at him, asking Thorn, "Are you a gentleman?"

"You'd get conflicting answers to that question, I suspect."

"I won't ask Hearst," she said, laughing.

"It's just as well."

"All right, then. If you must."

In fact, against his own best interest, Thorn found that he had been looking forward to it. When he crooked his left arm, Angelina let her hand rest lightly on the inside of his elbow, and they started down the sidewalk toward her residence. Before they'd traveled half a block, though, both heard a familiar and abrasive voice cut through the torchlight and its dancing shadows on the thoroughfare.

"How many of you have the fortitude to stand up for yourselves and strike a blow for white supremacy?" it challenged. "Is there any man amongst you who will fight?" An angry chorus of assent responded, echoing from the façades of structures on the thoroughfare.

"Damn it!"

Hearing the lady curse still took Thorn by surprise. "You'd better get on home now," he advised.

"Like hell I will!" she snapped, taking her notebook and a pencil from her purse, retreating toward the sound of voices at the south end of New Egypt.

Thorn caught up with her, saying, "This is a bad idea."

"It's *my* idea. My job!"

Rather than grab her forcibly and cause a scene, he kept pace with her, closing in on where the backwards-collared shouter they'd seen earlier was railing at another, larger crowd. Some members of his audience held torches now, while others carried pick handles and other makeshift bludgeons.

"You know where the trouble dwells!" he bellowed. "Where it seethes and multiplies in hatred and contempt of all things pure, all things *white!*"

"We know, by God!" somebody shouted from the crowd.

"What will you *do* about it, friends and neighbors?" asked the snake charmer.

" 'Neighbors'?" Angelina echoed, furiously. "If he lives in town or anyplace nearby, I'll eat my bonnet."

"Well," Thorn said, "there's still the Silver Crown."

"Damn Hearst!"

Thorn saw a deputy standing away to one side of the mob and asked, "Shouldn't your marshal be here?"

"Yes, he should." She looked around, scowling as she discovered Rockwell nowhere to be seen. "I won't forget this, either, letting down New Egypt when it needed him."

"Maybe he's on his way," Thorn said, uncertain why he made excuses for the lawman.

"Too late," Angelina said. "They're on *their* way, too."

The mob was moving off providing all its own noise now, in the direction of Celestial Alley. Thorn saw the supposed preacher watching as his furious disciples trooped away. Smiling, he stepped down from his crate and ducked into a nearby alley's mouth.

"You want to follow him?" asked Angelina.

"And do what? Chastise him?"

"Find out who he is! See who he's working for, as if we didn't know."

"I'd have to beat it out of him," Thorn said, not doubting it would work. "And then, what? Go to jail on an assault charge?"

"But—"

"Besides," he interrupted her, "your story's there." He pointed toward the torch-lit, snarling mob.

She hesitated, then replied, "Okay. Let's go!"

SOUTH OF NEW EGYPT

"Remember, now, we keep this quick and clean," Clete Alford told the other mounted Pinkertons.

"Well, quick, at least," one of them answered back, some of the others sniggering.

"Someone gets hurt or falls, we pick 'im up, no matter what," said Alford. "No one's left behind."

"No problem," said another of the team. "It's just a bunch a lazy Messicans."

"They could be armed," said Alford.

"Screw 'em," said the sneering rider. "I ain't never seen a Messican could shoot straight, anyhow."

The camp, with half a dozen fires burning, lay fifty yards in front of them, moonlight revealing tents and shanties patched together out of anything the striking miners could retrieve and use to build their makeshift homes. The hovels that had stovepipes were producing fragrant smoke. Alford smelled good things cooking, wished he could partake of them instead of riding roughshod over people who had done nothing to him.

To hell with that, a voice said in his mind. *It's what you're paid for.*

Mr. Hearst wanted the Belle Aire's striking miners swept away, and what he wanted was the same as God's command. He hadn't specified that any should be killed, but neither had he ruled it out. "Elimination" was the term Alford recalled, by any means required.

"All ready, then?" he called out softly, trying not to rouse the Mexicans before his raiders were among them, knocking over hovels, maybe setting fire to some, riding down whoever tried to run and wasn't quick enough to get out of their way. Along the ten-man skirmish line, he saw some nod, while others lifted hands to indicate they were prepared.

Most of the raised hands held six-guns.

Clete drew his own, hoping he wouldn't have to use it but for firing in the air, as if they were stampeding cattle. While a killer in his own right, he was not like some of those who rode with him, drawing enjoyment from it when they dropped the hammer on a man, woman, or child. He nearly laughed sometimes, when headquarters called them "detectives," then remembered who was paying him and choked it down.

One thing Clete *never* did was bite the hand that fed him, even when whatever he was eating tasted foul. Better to do what he was told and fatten as a parasite, the way of people everywhere in his experience, than find himself adrift and hungry, shut out in the cold.

Tonight's job would be running off the Mexicans, and that was what he meant to do.

Whisky was waiting for him at the Silver Crown, in case he needed it to help him sleep.

"Move in," he told the rest.

They started at a slow trot, staying more or less in line, their hoofbeats pattering on hard-packed desert soil, then broke into a lazy gallop, only stretching out full-speed within the last ten yards or so before they hit the outskirts of the camp.

A lookout shouted something to his friends in Spanish just before a pistol shot rang out and put him down. That stilled a couple of guitars that had been playing somewhere in the camp, and all Clete heard before his riders started whooping like a bunch of madmen was a baby's high-pitched squeal.

CELESTIAL ALLEY

The riot had a fair head start when Thorn and Angelina reached the scene, white men and yellow brawling on the thoroughfare and farther back into the alley, dark now in the absence of its normal hanging lamps, as if its occupants had braced themselves for violence.

And from what Thorn saw, the Chinese were delivering as good as what they got from the invaders. Some of them were armed with long poles, others swinging shorter clubs and chains, at least one brandishing a cleaver that had probably seen bloody action in the slaughterhouse. The whites had torches, pick handles, and anything that came to hand, some of them scooping rocks up from the unpaved street and lobbing them against the tight ranks of defenders.

Breaking through the front lines of Chinese seemed difficult, and Thorn was hoping that would hold until the law arrived, if Marshal Rockwell bothered to bestir himself, but then a pistol fired, immediately followed by two more. Those shots came from the white contingent, fired into the alley almost blindly, but the second volley came from inside there, the muzzle flashes winking, six or seven weapons blasting at the hostile racist crowd.

"Oh, God!" A gasp from Angelina, and he dragged her to the meager shelter of a shop's doorway nearby. Thorn saw a white man down—no, make that two—and then a couple more came limping from the hard heart of the action, clutching bloody wounds.

It had the makings of a massacre, and Thorn was wondering what he could do about it when he saw three men in dark suits moving down the sidewalk on the far side of the thoroughfare. All three had pistols drawn and wore the same grim-set expressions on their faces.

"Pinkertons!" said Angelina, straining in his grasp, but Thorn prevented her from rushing out to meet the gunmen.

"Stay here," he commanded, pushing her against the door for emphasis, then turned and jogged across the street to intercept the new arrivals.

Focused as they were, the gunmen hadn't seen him coming when he called out to them, "No one needs you here."

They turned as one to face Thorn, their apparent spokesman smiling as he answered back, "We'll be the judge of that."

"I don't think so," Thorn said.

"Don't give a shit what you think," said the mouth-piece, and their pistols rose as one.

Not fast enough.

Thorn drew both Colts and fired to wound them, if he could, though in the heat of battle there would be no guarantees. Completely ambidextrous, from handwriting to use of firearms, he squeezed off two shots per Peace-maker before the men confronting him could manage one. They lurched and fell, all hit—one in the leg, another in a shoulder, while the talker had a bullet somewhere in his torso.

"Stay down, now!" Thorn cautioned them, advancing with a mind to kick their guns beyond arm's reach. Before he reached them, though, the leader of the trio levered up on all fours, holding out his sidearm with a trembling hand.

"Son of a bitch!" he cried, thumbing its hammer back.

Thorn shot him in the chest, no time or inclination left for winging him. The thug died on his knees and toppled over backwards, slowly, to produce a cloud of dust on impact with the ground.

"You others done?" Thorn asked, and when they both stayed silent, moved in close enough to boot their guns away.

Behind him, with the riot still continuing, he heard a grim, familiar voice warn him, "That's goddamn far enough!"

SOUTH OF NEW EGYPT

The camp was screaming, smoking chaos. Everywhere he turned, Clete Alford saw dark shapes of men, women, and children running, seeking cover, while at least a dozen of their shoddy, thrown-together hovels burned. He thought he heard somebody howling in the midst of one pyre, but he didn't want to think about it, rode on by and didn't wait to catch a whiff of roasting meat.

The other boys were running wild, so far unscathed by any of the scattered shots fired in resistance. Mexicans of every shape and size were fleeing, more concerned with finding cover, getting out of pistol range, than fighting for what passed as dwellings in the camp. A part of Alford felt pathetic, joining in the rout, but at the same time he was jacked up on the primal thrill of battle, getting into it. He'd fired his six-gun twice so far, one miss, and on the second shot he'd seen a slender figure fall but didn't linger to assess the target's state.

His first hint of a problem came from overhead, how far he couldn't say. It was a screeching sound, reminding Alford of a hawk swooping on prey, but so much louder that it stung his ears and felt like nails piercing his skull. A moment later came a *whoosh* of something massive soaring past, no more than twenty, thirty feet above the desert floor, and he looked up to see a nightmare shadow blotting out the moon and stars.

"The hell?" he blurted out to no one, reining in his red dun mare and watching as the thing swept overhead, then dipped and came down close behind one of his riders. Was it Mack Bodine or Johnny Gray? He couldn't tell before a clawed foot closed around the horseman's head and yanked him from his saddle, hoisting him aloft while his mount galloped free.

Clete tried to follow where the monster went, but it was in a climbing spiral, great wings flapping, climbing up and up into the night sky. Seconds later, Alford's man came tumbling back to earth, but Clete got the impression there was only *part* of him. The body, what there was of it, crashed feet-first through the thin roof of a shack and vanished, four decrepit walls folding on top of it.

Alford was still trying to make sense of what he had seen, when once again he heard the screech—this time a little throatier, as if something was working down the creature's gullet. Horrified to think what that might be, he waved his pistol at the stars, seeking a target, and called out to his survivors, "Watch the sky, goddamn it! Something's—"

And before he could say "up there," it had dipped again, grabbing a second rider from his animal and sweeping him away. That one, Clete knew, was Arnie Gallagher, his wide-brimmed hat a giveaway. Arnie screamed once, then Alford heard a crunching noise that could have been an axe striking a watermelon but was not, and his dead friend made no more sounds.

The pattern was repeated, climb and spiral, nearly out of sight, before a tumbling partial body plummeted to land inside the camp. Gallagher missed the humble dwellings that still stood, thudding to earth and sending out a spume of fluid that was inky-black by moonlight.

"Jesus!" Alford cried, then hollered to the others, "Run! For God's sake, run!"

And suiting action to his words, he fled as if the world was ending—which, for all he knew, it was. Behind him, he heard gunshots popping in the camp, voices shouting in Spanish and in English, all the while praying to some god he'd forgotten since his childhood that he wouldn't hear the sound of wings racing along his track.

THIRTEEN

NEW EGYPT: JULY 16, 1875

Instead of staying with his men to quell the riot, Marshal Rockwell instantly relieved Thorn of his guns and marched him to New Egypt's jail, locked him inside one of its cells, both otherwise unoccupied, and left him there alone. During their walk back from the riot scene, Rockwell had stubbornly refused to hear from Angelina Farnum, parroting the phrase "I seen him shoot those men" until she gave up in disgust and went back to the locus of her latest front-page story, calling out to Thorn, "I'll be back soon."

In jail, Thorn waited till the first gray light of day came through the marshal's office windows, then Rockwell returned with Angelina on his heels, still nagging him. They cleared the threshold, Angelina telling the lawman, "You *can't* hold Gideon for self-defense against three gunmen when they'd threatened him."

"We'll let the circuit judge decide that," Rockwell snapped.

"And when does that old drunk come round again?"

"Should be in three, four weeks."

"You idiot!" she fairly screamed. "Those men were trying to kill Gideon!"

"You say. Sure didn't look that way to me."

"You notice that they all had guns in hand before he fired?"

"Well—"

"And that they were heading for the riot when he interrupted them?"

"That's not his job. It's mine."

"So, where in hell were *you*, Seth?"

"Listen, Mis—"

"Dare call me 'missy' and you'll have to put me in that other cell, for punching you!"

"Now, Angelina..."

"Can't you tell that they were Pinkertons? No different than that phony preacher stirring up the riot. You remember him, Seth? You were thrilled to guarantee his grand freedom of speech."

"I can't just overlook—"

"You pick and choose what you can overlook, Seth Rockwell. And I'm not the only one in town who's getting sick of it. You should have Hearst in here, asking him why he had gunmen at the riot scene after one of his lackeys set the ball rolling, but since you won't do that—"

"He's a respected—"

"Since you won't do *that*," she bulled ahead, "get used to seeing this on every front page of *The Hieroglyph* until your gin-soaked judge shows up, and then I'll add him to the list. Before I'm done with you—"

"For God's sake, Angelina, stop! What do you *want*?"

She stabbed a finger toward the cell where Thorn sat watching, smiling from his swaybacked cot. "I want him out of there, for starters, and whatever stupid charge you had in mind dismissed. I want you face to face with Hearst about his gunslingers, doing the job you were elected for. I want...well, we can hold it there for now. I'm bound to think of something else later."

Rockwell shook his head. Thorn couldn't tell if he was more disgusted with the woman or himself, but finally he nodded, staring at his boots. "All right, I'll wipe the slate on Thorn, since you're his witness and I trust you. As to Hearst—"

"Seth, if you don't—"

"I can't just haul him in here like a common criminal because *you* say some of his men were at the riot."

"You can *question* him, for Christ's—"

"Stop *swearing* at me, woman! Jumpin' Jesus Christ!"

"You set a fine example," Angelina told him, sounding smug.

"You know Hearst's reputation. He's a friend of governors and higher-ups all over the United States, including Richard Coke in Austin. If he raises Hob about me actin' up with him, you'll likely have another marshal by this time next week—and one he hand-picked for himself, maybe a Pinkerton."

"But Seth—"

"Besides, he'll just say that he's not his workers' keeper and he doesn't follow them around on their time off. You *know* he won't admit skullduggery against celestials or anybody else."

"Well..." Angelina's shoulders slumped. Thorn saw her giving in, but she soon rallied. "Then so be it. If his snake oil salesman has the freedom to start riots, I can run a series on the 'great man' who's behind him."

"Angelina—"

"Save your breath. Gideon's warned me Hearst might start a paper of his own and run me out of town. Before he gets the chance, I plan to scorch his tail feathers."

"This won't end well, I promise you," the marshal said.

"My paper, my lookout."

Nodding, Rockwell retrieved an outsized ring with two keys dangling from it, opened up Thorn's cell, and waved him toward his gunbelt resting on the marshal's desk.

"Try not to shoot nobody for a while," he groused. "Or have the lady for a witness if you do."

THE PYRAMID

"I'm disappointed in you, Raynard," Hearst said. "*Gravely* disappointed."

Dunn blinked and began to say, "It wasn't my—"

"Fault?" his employer finished for him. "Isn't that what you were just about to say? 'It wasn't my fault, Mr. Hearst'?"

"Or maybe 'sir'."

"You had one job. To stoke the fire and come back for your second payment when Celestial Alley *is no more.* Do you recall those words of mine?"

"Yes, sir."

"And is it standing, Raynard?"

"Well..."

"A simple 'yes' or 'no' will do."

"Yes."

"Yes, *what?*"

"Yes, sir, it's still standing. Or the bulk of it, at least. One of the laundries burned, I think."

"You *think?*"

"Because I left when it got rolling with the mob."

"You ran away."

"No, sir. I—"

"What?"

"The law was there."

"The law. And then three of my men—your friends, presumably—were shot, one of them killed."

"By Thorn, the newcomer."

Hearst froze on hearing that. "Gideon Thorn."

"I just heard 'Thorn'. The marshal took him in."

"To jail?"

"Yes, sir."

A knocking at the door distracted both of them. Hearst shouted, "Enter," frowning until Clete Alford came in. The baron's face lightened a little as he said, "Ah. Further news. Raynard, leave us."

Dunn headed for the door, then stopped as Hearst commanded, "Minus my five hundred dollars."

Dunn removed a bankroll from his pocket, handed it to Hearst, and said, "I done spent twenty of it, sir."

"Then I want *thirty* back by noon, if you intend to keep on working with the Pinkertons. Get out!"

He turned to Alford then, asking, "What word from south of town?"

"We had a problem, sir."

"What *kind* of problem, Clete?"

The gunman swallowed hard, then said, "The hungry flying kind."

"Explain yourself!"

"We hit the camp just like you said, sir. It was goin' fine

153

at first, and then there comes this racket overhead, and somethin' flies down, pickin' off our men. It snatched up Mack Bodine and Arnie Gallagher, one at a time, and took 'em up, tore pieces off a them, and dropped them back again, stone dead."

"You're babbling, man!"

"No, sir. I swear to God Almighty on a stack of Bibles."

"Spare me the theatrics. When you say a *thing,* what did it look like? Be specific."

"It was big, real big, with wings thirty or forty feet across. It's head was pointy-like, I'd say, and mebbe six feet long, claws big enough to grab a man off horseback and just carry him away, nearly straight up."

"A *monster,* then. Is that your story?"

"I don't know what else you'd call it, sir."

"And who else saw this vision?"

"All the riders that come back alive with me, plus all them Messicans."

Hearst crossed the suite to his wet bar, poured half a water glass full of rye whisky, and immediately drank it down in two long swallows, grimacing as it scalded his throat.

"Jesus, the shit I listen to from idiots," he told the room at large. Turning to Alford once again, he asked, "You swear to me that story is the truth, knowing your very life depends on it?"

"Yes, sir! I'd tell a better one if I could think of any, but it's gospel true."

"A flying monster," Hearst murmured. "A *dragon.* Was it breathing fire, by any chance?"

"No, sir. Just eatin' men."

"All right. Go home, by which I mean the Silver Crown

and nowhere else. I have an errand to take care of at the jail."

"Yes, sir."

At least the shooting of Hearst's Pinkertons downtown couldn't be blamed on any creature from a fantasy. The man who'd killed them was behind bars, and if Hearst could swing it, he'd be seeing Thorn dance on the gallows one day soon.

As for the Mexicans, the monster, and the rest of it, all that required more thought.

NEW EGYPT MARSHAL'S OFFICE

Gideon Thorn was buckling his pistol belt when Marshal Rockwell's door flew open and George Hearst entered the office like a thunderstorm on legs.

"Marshal," the mining boss began to say, then saw Thorn standing by the desk and armed, demanding, "What in hell is going on here?"

Instead of spilling everything at once, Rockwell responded with a question of his own. "What's your concern, sir?"

"My *concern?* I've just been told that three of my employees have been shot, one of them killed, by *this* man." His accusing finger aimed at Thorn. "Word had it that you'd locked him up, and rightly, but I see now that he's fancy free!"

At that point, Angelina Farnum broke into the conversation, pencil poised above her notepad. "You admit the three were your employees, then?"

Hearst glowered, turning red. "I will not be interrogated by—"

"That's fine," she interrupted him. "I got it down the first time."

Hearst turned back toward Rockwell. "Marshal, why is this assassin—"

"Speaking of assassins," Angelina butted in, "why were your gunmen standing by Celestial Alley with their pistols drawn, during a race riot?"

Trying to ignore her, Hearst told Seth, "My three employees were off-duty at the time, Marshal. Their free time is their own, like any other man's. That does not give *this* person liberty to gun them down like dogs."

"I doubt that dogs would try to kill him," Angelina said, "thus forcing him to fire in self-defense."

"Preposterous!" Hearst raged. "Defamatory nonsense."

"Jurors will decide that when I testify in court," she said, "assuming there's a charge that goes to trial."

"There's no charge at the moment," Rockwell said to all those present.

"One man dead, two wounded, and *no charge?*"

"You also have a fourth man missing, Mr. Hearst," said Angelina.

"Do I, now?"

"The fellow with the backwards collar on," she said, "who was lambasting the Chinese today, downtown. Coincidentally, he showed up for a second time, minutes before the riot, then went slinking down an alley close to your hotel."

"Madam," Hearst replied stiffly, "I have no earthly notion what you're saying, but unless you have some proof, printing that kind of twaddle can be dangerous."

"A threat?" she challenged him.

"Of litigation, absolutely."

Thorn, watching the argument with interest, confidently said, "He's lying through his beard."

Hearst rounded on him, sneering, "Says the *killer*, whom our *marshal* has seen fit to set at liberty. Whatever you may think of me, this town's corruption—"

"That's enough!" said Rockwell, getting in the tycoon's face. "If you have a complaint to file, get on with it. If not, I have a riot to investigate, and those associated with it."

Hearst was shorter than the lawman, but his rigid stance seemed to increase his height. "Complaints to you would clearly be a waste of time. I may, however, send one of my several attorneys to the sheriff in Fort Davis."

"I imagine they're already well acquainted," Rockwell answered, through clenched teeth.

Glancing from Thorn to Angelina, Hearst said, "Marshal, you have backed a losing horse in this race. Two, I should say: one wild bronco and a nag."

Before Rockwell could think of a response, a man Thorn hadn't seen before barged through the office doorway Hearst had left wide open. He was short and hefty, nearly out of breath from rushing down the thoroughfare.

"Marshal!" he gasped. "There's trouble with the Mexicans, in camp."

Thorn caught Hearst giving the excited messenger a sidelong glance, frowning, raising a hand to stroke his beard.

"What kinda trouble," Seth inquired.

"All kinds of hell. Somebody hit the camp last night, around the same time as that trouble with the Chinks. They've got some houses burnt, if you can call 'em that, and people shot."

"Shot by who?" the marshal pressed him.

"Raiders. No one knows for sure. But worst of all—"

"There's more?"

"The Mexicans are sayin' some kind of a flyin' monster came in while the rest of it was goin' on, kilt two of 'em that was attackin' and ate parts of 'em."

"Jesus!" Seth shook his head. "That thing again."

"Yessir. Just thought you oughta know, in case...well...I'll be goin' now."

Three pairs of eyes settled on Hearst. "A raid against the Mexicans," said Rockwell. "Mr. Hearst, would you know anything about that, for the record?"

"I would not! And it's insulting that you even ask me such a question!" Hearst huffed back at him. "I'm leaving now, unless you have more foolish inquiries?"

"Not yet," Seth said. "But I know where to find you if I do."

When Hearst was gone, Rockwell turned back to Thorn and Angelina, slumping with his backside resting on his desk, and heaved a weary sigh. "There's no such thing as gentle rain," he said. "It only pours."

"Seth," Angelina answered, "I believe the proper saying is—"

He waved her off. Said, "I don't need you tellin' me my speech is wrong, right now."

"Sorry." She seemed to mean it, blushing.

"Mr. Thorn," Seth said, "I never thought I'd say this, but I have a problem now—two, really—and I may need someone's help."

"Besides your deputies?" asked Thorn.

The lawman shook his head. "They've got the same trouble I do, which at the moment is our jurisdiction."

"Ah." Gideon thought he saw where this was going.

"First, whatever happened to the Mexicans, they're camped outside of town," Seth said. "I've got no more legal authority out there than you or anybody else. I'll send Isaiah Kent and Dr. Gilmore out, if they agree to go, and I can take an unofficial look around—I should, in fact, in case the trouble spreads back here to town—but far as makin' an investigation, that's the county sheriff's bailiwick, if he decides to come and deal with it."

"But if someone already has the sheriff in his pocket..." Angelina said, leaving the thought unfinished.

"Then, he'll either turn a blind eye to it," Rockwell said, "or claim to find whatever he's been told to."

Thorn had dealt with city-county conflicts in the past. Now he told Rockwell, "If you want someone to ride out there and ask some questions, I've already met César Estrada."

"Figured that you might've," Seth replied. "I can't request it of you, can't even advise it, but I won't say 'no'."

"Thanks, Marshal."

"For what?" Not waiting for an answer, Rockwell forged ahead. "Another problem, on the same lines, is the fella with the dog collar from yesterday."

"He was in town," said Angelina. "You saw him, yourself, and so did we." A gesture of her hand included Thorn. "If he's still here—"

"That's just the trouble," Rockwell cut her off. "*If* he's still somewhere in New Egypt, I would have to rate him as a fool. And if he *is* that dumb, I know damn well Hearst isn't. Either way, I'm guessin' he's skedaddled outa here by now. The question is, *to where?*"

Thorn didn't have to ponder that. "We pegged him for a Pinkerton," he said. "If true, he's only got two choices: leave the area completely or head out to join his cronies at the Silver Crown."

"My guess would be the mine," said Angelina.

"And again, outside my jurisdiction," Rockwell said.

"But if someone went out to have a look and saw him there," Thorn said, "and maybe made a citizen's arrest..."

"That's every person's right, if they can pull it off," Seth granted. "But that someone oughta be damned careful, sniffin' around all those Pinkertons."

Thorn nodded. "I was out there once before. Nobody spotted me."

"But you weren't grabbing one of them."

"Point taken."

"I'll be going with you to the camp," said Angelina. "Never mind the arguments. Newspapers don't have jurisdictions."

"Might still be dangerous," Seth said, plainly concerned.

"I'm going," she repeated.

"Right. Okay."

"Well, if we're going soon..." Thorn left it there.

"You'll want to stop at the hotel, I guess," said Rockwell. "We can meet up at the livery in, what? Say fifteen minutes?"

Thorn's nod sealed the deal.

"One other thing," the marshal said, turning to Angelina. "I want to apologize for...all of this."

"Seth, you can't change the laws," she said.

"It ain't just that. The whole way I been actin' for the past few days..."

"No, honestly."

Thorn felt like an intruder, eavesdropping upon a moment meant for two alone. He stepped around the pair of them and left the office, striding down the sidewalk toward The Pyramid. He would reclaim his Winchester, maybe the Sharps as well, and pay a visit to the famous water closet before hiking down to fetch Shadow.

Whatever happened at César Estrada's camp, he meant to be prepared.

FOURTEEN

SOUTH OF NEW EGYPT

Seven of them rode out to the camp: Thorn on his stallion; Rockwell and a deputy he brought along as witness; Angelina in a rented buggy; Dr. Gilmore riding in the undertaker's wagon, with a helper Kaiser had retained for any heavy lifting. Something like a dozen townspeople had tried to tag along, but Seth discouraged them in no uncertain terms.

The camp, as they'd been cautioned to expect, was in a state of chaos. Smoke hovered over all, assaulting Thorn's nostrils with the aromas of burnt wood, tarpaper, maybe flesh and hair. He didn't want to think about that at the moment, as they met the posted guards and Rockwell asked to see César Estrada.

Two men armed with ancient pistols kept them company, while a companion ran to fetch the camp's *de facto* leader. Thorn tried to ignore the passing time as they sat waiting, finally relieved to see Estrada coming toward them with the runner. César had a bandage wrapped around his head, a portion of it near his hairline decorated with a rusty stain.

The first words from Estrada's lips were, "You do not belong here, *mariscal*. We are not in New Egypt."

"Nope," Rockwell replied. "Me and my deputy are only here to see the damage, private like, and ask if you need any help."

Estrada frowned suspiciously. "Some of my people have been injured by *los hombres blancos* who attacked us in the night," he said. "Others are dead."

"White men," Thorn said, in case the others hadn't translated the comment.

"Got it," Rockwell said. Then, to Estrada, "Dr. Gilmore might be able to assist your wounded. Mr. Kaiser is our undertaker, if you need help with the folks who didn't make it."

"We shall bury them ourselves," Estrada said. "Before we leave."

"You're leaving?" Angelina asked him. "Going where, if I may ask?"

"Back home, to Mexico," César replied. "We have tried Texas and it is not to our liking."

"Well, I'm sorry to hear that," the marshal interjected.

"Why?" Estrada challenged him. "You'd rather have us stay and work for pennies at the Belle Aire Mine?"

"That ain't my business here this morning," Seth replied, "or any other time. I've got nothin' to do with Boone or Hearst."

Estrada's frown was skeptical. He asked, "Rich men don't own the law?"

"They *make* the laws, most of the time," Rockwell acknowledged. "And they own some that enforce it. I'm not one of 'em."

"Come with me, then," César said, "as private citizens. I show your doctor to my injured. You can see the rest, and take the two dead *asaltantes* with you, if you want them."

Rockwell glanced at Thorn, who told him, "That means 'raiders'."

"If they're Pinkertons, I'll need to have more words with Hearst," Seth said.

Thorn frowned. Replied, "If we can even tell."

He thought about the mangled body from Celestial Alley, named by Hearst as one of his after the fact. A pattern had emerged, but Thorn suspected it was nothing anyone could prove in court.

The camp reminded Thorn of photographs he'd seen, depicting battlefields during the Civil War, albeit on a smaller scale. Burned shacks were hardly comparable to whole cities torched in wartime, but he recognized that living, breathing people had inhabited the structures, some spending the last days of their lives there, all expecting to have futures, hoping that the months and years ahead would be more joyful than their past in troubled Mexico. The sound of weeping women pierced him, making Thorn wish he could plug his ears or turn off his emotional response to so much suffering. His face revealed nothing as they rode deeper into César's camp, but he missed nothing with his eyes.

When he glanced to his left, at Angelina in her buggy, she looked stunned, tears brimming in her eyes, her hands white-knuckled on the horse's reins.

They reached a tent larger than most that had survived the raid, apparently set up for treatment of Estrada's wounded countrymen. Arriving there, the undertaker's wagon stopped and Dr. Gilmore scrambled down, his heavy leather bag in hand, waving the others off as he got down to work.

"Perhaps he helps them," César said, not fully seeming to believe it. "Now, for those who are not healers, let us see the dead."

SILVER CROWN MINE

"You both screwed up, is what I'm telling you," said Otis Breen.

"How'n the hell did *I* screw up?" fumed Raynard Dunn.

"You had your orders," Breen replied. "Tell me if they were carried out."

Dunn hesitated for a beat, then said, "I did *my* part, all right. Can't help it if them other three got shot messin' around before *their* bit was done. The rest, I had no orders to wade in and show the stupid townies what to burn or stop 'em gettin' scared by the celestials."

"Tell that to Mr. Hearst," Breen said.

"I did. He sent me back out here."

"And here you are." Breen turned to face Clete Alford. "As for you—"

"Don't lump me in with *him,*" said Alford, jutting out his bristly chin toward Dunn. "He didn't have no flyin' monster pickin' off his men and eatin' 'em like they was shrimp."

"You're still on that?" Breen asked, half sneering.

"That's exac'ly what I saw," Clete said.

"Well, God help both of you," Breen said, turned on his heel, and went back to his shack outside the Silver Crown's adit, where Cornishmen were busy their work.

Both Pinkertons watched him retreat, then Dunn, minus his phony parson's collar, said, "I'm thinkin' I might just as well light out."

"Hearst tell you that?"

"I'm thinkin' for myself."

"Well, I'd think twice," Alford replied. "He might not care, but on the other hand, if he's got work for you to do and you ain't here..."

"The hell's he gonna do?"

"Reach out first to Chicago. If you up and quit the Eye, he'll likely toss a coin, decide if you're worth chasin' down to wherever you're runnin'."

"He don't own the whole damn world!"

"Nope. But his money's got a long, *long* reach."

"Shit fire! What're *you* gonna do?"

"Sit tight, at least for now. I think he half believes me. Now I wait'n see if he cooks up another plan."

"Well, you know he ain't backin' off. When did he ever?"

"Never once I heard of," Clete agreed.

"There's bound to be more blood."

"As long as it ain't ours," Clete said, including Dunn although he didn't really give a damn about the mouth-piece known for riling mobs and tricking enemies of Hearst to break the law, so they could be arrested and locked up.

"Amen to that," Dunn said. And then, "About that monster..."

"I already told you what it looked like, more or less. I couldn't see no more."

"I was just wonderin' how somethin' like that came to be," said Dunn.

"You need to ask somebody else. I ain't no zookeeper."

Dunn changed directions. "We've lost, what? Six men, now?"

"Four dead. Two more wounded, maybe facin' charges."

"Damn. I never seen a Pinkerton arrested. You?"

"The marshal in New Egypt's got a screw loose," Alford said. "He's gonna buck the old man? That'll be his last mistake."

"Maybe. Back to the monster for a second."

"Jesus, Dunn!"

"In case it comes out here again, like Wednesday night," said Raynard. "D'you think the Gatlin' gun can stop it?"

Alford let his eyes drift toward the wagon with its big gun gleaming, heating in the sunshine. "Well," he said at last, "truth is, I don't have a goddamn idea. If we can hit it, maybe so. I seen it fly, though, and the way it rolls around, dippin' and soarin' in the air, it's like a pigeon. If a pigeon weighed a couple tons and ate people."

Dunn might have shuddered, but Clete wasn't sure and didn't care. He craved a whisky, maybe three, but Mr. Hearst was coming out later and wouldn't tolerate the smell of liquor on an agent's breath, unless he was off duty.

"Gonna get some sleep," he told Dunn, turning toward the bunkhouse. "I been up all night and got a feelin' there'll be worse to come."

SOUTH OF NEW EGYPT

Seven Mexicans had died outright in the attack. Five had been shot, three of them in the back while fleeing from their killers. One, a child Thorn couldn't recognize as boy or girl, had been trampled beneath a horse's hooves, grossly disfigured. The last one, burned to a blackened crisp, had been incinerated in one of the shacks.

Angela was dabbing at her eyes with a lace handkerchief, switching it for her pencil as she scribbled shorthand notes about the grisly scene. She said nothing at first, but listened raptly as César Estrada told his story of the raid, white men on horseback charging, shooting, knocking over those who tried to get away. The gunmen had not carried torches. Rather, it appeared that the burned hovels caught fire after they were toppled in the midst of paltry dinner preparations for their occupants.

"We had guards posted," César said. "Guillermo Aguillar, just there, was shot down when he tried to keep the raiders out. The rest are as you see."

"Who was the child?" asked Angelina, tight-voiced.

"Franzea Vargas. She was five years old."

Thorn noticed Angelina bite her lip as she was jotting down the information, taking César through the names of murdered comrades one by one. When that was done, he asked, "You want to see the *gringos* now?"

The two dead raiders had been set apart from members of the camp who'd lost their lives. Approaching them, walking Shadow, Thorn saw that they had suffered damage similar to Jed Tabor, buried the day before on New Egypt's Boot Hill. Neither was perfectly identical, but they were similar enough—great ragged wounds excising heads and shoulders, one arm in the first case, both gone from the other—that he had no qualms about blaming one killer for all three.

"Like Tabor," Rockwell said, framing Thorn's thoughts in words.

"What does this?" Angelina asked, standing in awe.

"We have three dead we're sure of, two descriptions of

the killer," Thorn replied. "They're all the same, or close enough for me, at least. Unless you want to tell me someone ripped these shooters with a crosscut saw and no one saw him do it, all the while flying some kind of giant kite over two different murder scenes, I'm going with the monster."

"Goddamn dragon," Rockwell said.

"Until we have a better name for it," Thorn said.

"Well, that beats all."

"Not us," said Angelina. "We're not beaten yet."

"I don't know about you two," Rockwell said, "but I don't have a plan for this."

"That's why we need to make one," Thorn replied.

"What do we do?" the lawman challenged him. "Try shootin' it? Get lassoes on it, try'n bring it down? And then what? Sure as hell, it won't fit in the jail. And if it busted out the Belle Aire Mine, a barn won't hold it, neither."

Thorn already had his mind made up the creature had to die. Whatever it might be, what ever niche it once had filled in nature, it was nothing but a menace now. They couldn't pen it up or carry it into the wilderness for safe release, like some rogue wolf of bear. The thing was huge, and it could *fly*. It was a man-eater, confirmed by three half-corpses and the missing Chan Li Gong. If they surveyed the neighborhood, who else was missing that they didn't know about?

"We'll think about a weapon," he told Rockwell. "In the meantime, it's important that we limit its resources."

"Meaning what?" asked Angelina. "It's got all outdoors to hunt in."

"But it's come back twice to settlements, at least," Thorn said. "Maybe three times, if the dead man it dropped in Celestial Alley came from over at the Silver Crown."

"Hearst says that was a trick pulled off by Boone," Rockwell replied.

"Of course he would," said Angelina. "You believe him?"

"Lookin' at this mess," Seth said, "I don't know what'n hell to think."

César Estrada interrupted the debate, telling them all, "I saw *Quetzalcoatl* with my own eyes. If you don't believe me, then play games until he comes to feed on you."

"You told me earlier it burned to death, in legend, but that doesn't seem to be the case," Thorn said. "What are your thoughts on killing it?"

"To kill a god?" Estrada smiled and shook his head. "Who knows if that is even possible?"

"It lives and breathes. There has to be some way," said Angelina.

"If I knew that," Escobar replied, "we might try it, instead of going back to Mexico."

SILVER CROWN MINE

George Hearst found Otis Breen waiting to greet him when he stepped out of his trap, leaving the reins to dangle free. Breen's face looked pinched, as if he had bad news to share —the last thing that Hearst needed on this brutal day.

"They here?" he asked his manager.

"Clete is. Raynard took off about an hour ago."

"Where to?"

"I asked him. Wouldn't say. Told me to tell you, you can stuff your paycheck where the sun don't shine."

"That yellow bastard!"

"Knew what he was doing, anyway. We warned him there was nowhere he could hide."

"I'll prove that to him at my leisure. In the meantime, we have crises to control."

"I know about the mess in town, and at the greasers' camp," Breen said.

"That's only part of it," said Hearst. "That half-assed marshal, Rockwell, and the woman from the newspaper are both in league with Thorn, trying to implicate me in last night's events and any other crime their dim wits can conceive."

"Good luck to them, with Raynard gone," said Breen. "You know Clete isn't gonna squeal. He's hang a dozen times before they laid a glove on you."

"Not if he makes a deal to testify."

"You have too many well-placed friends, from Austin back to Washington."

"Forget the White House, Otis. Grant's mired in too many scandals of his own to spare a thought for me, from doubling his own salary to covering the Star Route postal ring, now with the trading post and whisky rings dragging him through the mud. You mark my words: our president's already looking forward to retirement with his fortune."

"What about the governor?" asked Breen.

"Coke's busy with the new state constitution, trying to disfranchise niggers while he's got the chance," Hearst said. "I have it on the best authority that he'll resign as soon as that's accomplished. Richard Hubbard's likely to replace him, but he mainly wants to be a senator."

"Buy the election," Breen suggested. "Pick your own man."

"That's a possibility," Hearst said. "But in the meantime, I need some way to stop Rockwell fitting me for a rope necktie."

"You think that's really possible?"

"Right now, Otis, I couldn't say."

"Then, if the marshal won't listen to reason, take him out. Won't be the first time."

"No, but he's on notice now. And there's that damned newspaper, not to mention Thorn. I told you he has solid money of his own?"

"You did. Back East."

"Not organized against us yet, but if we're seen to have a hand in getting rid of him..."

"Then let the monster do it, Boss," Breen said.

"The monster?" Hearst considered it, and then repeated thoughtfully, "The monster."

"It's a natural. Of course, to pull it off..."

"Requires more than a modicum of expertise. You're right, of course."

"I grant you, finding it and putting it to work for us could be a major problem."

"Or unnecessary," Hearst replied. "If Thorn should die, his passing only needs to *seem* as if it were the creature's work."

"Same means of mangle," Breen observed.

"Precisely. If he simply disappears while searching for it...well, then, who's to say what happened?"

"Perfect, Boss."

"In broad strokes," Hearst admitted. "But the Devil's in the details. If we don't get those in line..."

"We always do," Breen said, with total confidence.

"It only takes one slip-up."

"Planned out to perfection in advance."

"With no mistakes."

"Nary a one."

"I'll want to oversee each step along the way," Hearst said.

"Like always, Boss. Sure thing."

"All right. Give it some focused thought. I'll do the same."

"The marshal?" Breen reminded him. "And the newspaper?"

"I'll consult Mayor Neagle about putting Marshal Rockwell out to pasture," Hearst replied. "*The Hieroglyph* already has an article—or more than one—in preparation, naming me as an accomplice in the mayhem of last night and God knows what-all."

"Vile, malicious speculation," Breen said. "Slap them with a libel suit."

"Mud sticks, no matter how we try to brush it off, Otis."

"Then strike a match," Breen said. "Hotter mud gets, drier it is, sooner it blows away."

FIFTEEN

NEW EGYPT

The mood was grim in Rockwell's office when Thorn, the marshal, and Angelina Farnum returned from César Escobar's camp. Of the three, Angelina seemed most shaken by what she had seen, but she stayed focused on the prospect of reporting all about it in *The Hieroglyph*. Rockwell had poured himself a glass of whiskey from a bottle in his desk drawer, while the other two declined.

"All right," the lawman said when it was down his throat. "I guess we've got a monster."

"Either that," Thorn said, "or the most costly hoax in history."

"How many dead is that?" Seth asked. "From just this thing, I mean."

"I make it four, if we count Chan Li Gong," said Angelina.

"Prob'ly out there in the desert, somewhere," Rockwell said, "unless it ate him up entirely. Anybody figure why it dropped the others off, half-eaten?"

"Last night could have been excitement from the fires and shooting," Thorn suggested. "With the other Pinkerton, Tabor, I couldn't guess."

"Droppin' him over Celestial Alley, one night after pickin' up one of the Chinks."

"Seth, honestly." There was a weariness to Angelina's scolding voice. "After what we've just seen?"

"Sorry. It's habit, I suppose. A bad one."

"Try to break it, will you?" she admonished him.

Rockwell nodded, then asked, "Anybody got a plan on how to kill it yet?"

Thorn, seated in one of the office's two extra chairs, answered, "It's attacked three places that we know of: first, the Silver Crown, then on the alley in New Egypt, finally the camp outside of town. The camp, we know, is moving out before day's end."

"So what?" Seth asked.

"I can't predict its movements," Thorn replied, "but if *I* were the creature, and I started getting hungry, I'd go back to someplace where I caught a meal before."

Angelina got it. "The Silver Crown or Celestial Alley."

Thorn nodded. "I may be way off, but we can't guard everyplace at once. It makes sense, watching targets where it's gotten lucky in the past."

"The Chinks—*Chinese,* sorry—have got the alley covered, far as I can tell," Rockwell replied. "Between this thing and white men comin' down to burn 'em out, they're up in arms. No tellin' what all they're equipped with, but I wouldn't try to put a deputy in there right now. It's all his life is worth to set foot in the place."

"A twist on that," Thorn said, "if it's discouraged from the street itself, could be a run down through the midst of town."

"Christ, don't say that!" The lawman paled. "We'll have the whole damn settlement uprooted if that happens."

"I'm just saying it's a possibility."

"All right. I've got two deputies, and I can try to find some more to share the watch from dusk to sunrise, covering the thoroughfare at least."

"Avoid the rooftops," Thorn advised him. "No point offering this thing a free buffet."

"A what?"

"Free meal," translated Angelina. Shifting restlessly, she said, "I need to get back with this story now. I'm putting out an extra on it, and I've been no help to you."

"It helps, warning the people," Thorn suggested.

"Right. The ones who will believe it, anyway."

"At least, maybe they'll stay indoors," Seth said.

"Let's hope," she said, and left them with a sad-sounding good-bye.

When she was gone, Seth said, "Okay, we've got New Egypt covered, more or less, and Hearst still has his shooters at the Silver Crown."

"They weren't much help last time," Thorn said.

The marshal frowned. "What've you got in mind?"

"Another visit. Maybe help them watch over the place."

The lawman laughed at that, a bitter sound. "The way Hearst feels about you, that's a good way to get killed," he said.

Thorn shrugged, smiled. "Only if they catch me at it."

"Damn. I'd say you're better off with dragons, but I don't know which is worse."

"With any luck, we'll have them both in one place," Gideon replied.

"Well, it's your life. I can't stop you. But Angelina will be sad when you get shot or eaten up."

Thorn read Seth's tone and said, "There's nothing going on between us, Marshal. Well, this dragon thing, but that's the limit to it."

Rockwell slumped a little further in his chair. "Appreciate you sayin' that, not that it helps me any. Skippin' over it, you have some kinda plan?"

"So far," Thorn said, "this creature only seems to feed at night. I'll head out to the Silver Crown around sunset and should arrive just as it's getting dark. I have a place to watch from, where they didn't spot me last time. Hold up there and keep an eye out. If the thing comes hunting and the Pinkertons can't bring it down, weigh in the best I can."

"We know it isn't scared of Winchesters or six-guns, Gideon. Hearst has that Gatling out there, but it didn't help Jed Tabor."

"I can try my Sharps, the .50-90," Thorn suggested.

"That'll drop a buffalo—or elephant, I'm told—but this thing..."

"It's a gamble," Thorn admitted. "But it's all that I can think of."

"Okay, then," said Rockwell. "Try'n do your best to stay alive."

THE PYRAMID HOTEL

Thorn ate lunch at The Pyramid alone. Not knowing when —or if—he'd have another meal, he loaded up: a twenty-ounce tenderloin steak, a good-sized potato with garlic salt baked on its skin, and collared greens spiced up somehow by one of Aunt Lou's special recipes. Eating the feast, the dining room near empty after last night's grim events, Thorn had to wonder whether it would be his final meal.

At least, with her distraction at *The Hieroglyph*, he didn't have to worry about Angelina coming with him as they had originally meant for her to do.

The plan he'd hatched, if you could rightly call it that, was thin at best. Watching and waiting after nightfall for the flying beast to show itself, badly outnumbered by the Silver Crown's protective force of Pinkertons, might wind up a frustrating failure or, in the alternative, dish up a fresh disaster. The beast had managed to elude humans four times, counting its breakout from the Belle Aire Mine, and after facing guns three times, it showed no signs of weakening in last night's raid.

If anything, Thorn would have said that it was growing bolder, more aggressive.

Which spelled trouble for New Egypt, and for anyone who crossed its path thereafter, if it managed to escape again.

That posed another question for him that he couldn't answer: was it staying in the area simply to feed, or from familiarity, something about the place that held it there? Not knowing what it was, how long it had survived below, or where its forebears had originated, Thorn could only speculate. If instinct ruled the creature—homing, or perhaps even a mating urge—it would have found the landscape changed since it was last at liberty. Repopulated by a tasty but annoying race, New Egypt and environs offered it slim prospects for a peaceful life, and none at all for reproducing.

Thank God that it doesn't have a mate, he thought, and chewed another bite of steak. If there were any more, much less a swarm of hungry offspring to be fed...

It might have spelled disaster for the human race, or for that part of Texas, anyway. And if the Texan brand of opposition proved discouraging enough, it was a short flight down to Mexico—vast deserts, the Sierra Madre Oriental mountains, jungle farther south, and all the tiny villages a family of predators could ever need.

And could he stop that happening? What could a single man accomplish, when New Egypt and the Silver Crown were already protected by so many guns?

Nothing, perhaps, but Thorn was bound to try.

He hadn't come this far, chasing the nightmare of his infancy, to back off now. New Egypt's dragon had nothing to do with what had happened to his family, yet it was still part of his long, strange quest. If the frontier held deadly mysteries in store, Thorn's self-appointed, dedicated task was to reveal their secrets and, wherever possible, prevent them from disrupting human lives.

Some might have called that "noble," but he didn't think of it that way.

For Gideon, the long, perhaps unending hunt was simply *personal*.

THE HIEROGLYPH

Brandon Price wanted to run a newspaper someday. He also nursed a not-so-secret yen for Angelina Farnum, and she took advantage of him on both scores, enlisting him to help her with the paper at a low wage, supplementing his employment as a handyman, without encouraging any romantic fantasies.

Today, their project was a special printing of *The Hiero-*

glyph, alerting any residents who hadn't heard the story yet to last night's violent events. For those who'd heard some garbled version of the riot and the Pinkerton attack on hapless Mexicans in the Estrada camp, she aimed to set the record straight.

And that meant introducing New Egyptians to the monster from the Belle Aire Mine.

Most of them knew at least some portion of the story now, though many still dismissed it as a superstitious myth or hoax cooked up by miners going out on strike. The evidence of Angelina's own two eyes should disabuse them of that attitude, and for the skeptics who still passed it off as nothing...well, she would have done her best.

They had the type all plated and two copies printed out for proofreading, scanning from headlines down to smallest print for errors. There would be no advertisements in the extra, nothing but stark news of death and perfidy, including Angelina's take on the conspiracy to frighten Randolph Boone's former employees out of town. Would that line of attack lead her to court, defending libel charges against high-priced and experienced attorneys for the Hearst empire?

If so, she was prepared for that—or hoped she was, at any rate.

Meanwhile, there was a story to be told, and that was what she lived for. Angelina knew that she might never see another like it in her lifetime, even prayed that such would be the case, but she was living in the middle of it now and could not shirk her duties as a journalist.

Was that courageous? To a point, perhaps, but when she thought about the men who would be risking life and limb to stop the monster—Gideon, Seth Rockwell and his deputies—her part seemed almost trivial. Their battle would unfold whether she sold another round of newspapers or not, regardless of acceptance or denial on the part of local residents. The creature was *reality,* and only through its death would order be restored.

A pang of sadness at the thought lanced Angelina and surprised her. She knew nothing of the rogue monstrosity beyond the damage it had caused so far, yet part of her still grieved at the idea of its demise. It was a *special* thing, perhaps unique, and when it died—*if* they could kill it— what would happen then?

She pictured scientists, most likely from the East since Texas had no university as yet, descending on New Egypt to dissect and study something they had never seen before. Enhancing knowledge, they would call it, but for whom? Announcement of the creature's unexpected life and death would be a nine-day's wonder, might even establish Angelina as a star among her era's journalists, but it would fade in time. Some other curiosity would soon replace it in the public consciousness, while most of dull humanity plodded along, immersed in daily toil and private passions, heedless.

And to Angelina's mind it all played out the same, another death, heaped onto those that went before.

"I've got an error here," said Brandon, circling a short word on his proof sheet.

"Go ahead and fix the type," she ordered, barely glancing up at him.

When this was over, if she hadn't been sued into bankruptcy or jailed by some Texas judge for criminal libel, what came next? Her husband's dream, the newspaper, had proved infectious, but it wasn't rooted in New Egypt necessarily. If she survived the coming storm with reputation more or less intact, what would prevent her moving to a larger market, even out of Texas? Going back to Kansas City, with its two large papers and a host of smaller ones, was likely too ambitious, and she harbored no desire to be cover "ladies' issues" for a paper run by gruff old men. A taste of independence—and a leading role in what would surely be the most important story of the decade, possibly the century—had spoiled her for subordination to a stuffy editor convinced that he "knew best."

Or she could stay and build *The Hieroglyph*. Why not? The paper she had started with her husband as a one-page sheet had served her well enough so far.

But all of that was premature. The next few hours, days at most, would finally determine what became of Angelina, her endeavors, and the town itself. What would remain of all the hard work poured into New Egypt?

Who would even be alive?

THE PYRAMID HOTEL

At four-fifteen by Thorn's watch, George Hearst drove a buggy out of town and toward his mining claim. Thorn watched him pass by the hotel, no Pinkerton escort, then lay down on his bed to rest. A long night stretched ahead of him, and there was no way to predict when he would sleep again.

Hearst's presence at the Silver Crown increased Thorn's need for stealth while he surveilled the place. The Pinkertons would be on guard, of course, but mostly watching skyward, and there a tendency among many employees to be lax without the boss man watching every move they made. Whether the great man feared intruders of the human kind or not, by simply showing up on site he would heighten the need of his hired guns to prove themselves.

And that was bad for any lurker shadowing the mine.

As far as strategy, Thorn planned to find the same spot from which he had watched the Silver Crown, his first day in New Egypt. Covered by the night, he'd wait, using his spyglass, holding back unless the monster showed itself.

And then?

He had the Sharps, set up to kill at fifteen hundred yards, more than three-quarters of a mile away. Darkness and scattered lighting at the claim would compromise that range, but Thorn's selected post was under half that distance from the Silver Crown's adit and bunkhouse. It was doable, in theory, though a moving target on the wing, regardless of its size, increased his difficulty.

And if he could score a decent hit, what happened next?

The .50-90 Sharps black power cartridge packed a wallop. Its 440-grain bullets—twenty-nine grams apiece— flew down range at 1,749 feet per second, striking the target with 2,989 foot-pounds of destructive energy. No creature known to science could withstand it, but the point of impact made a crucial difference in how a hunter's prey reacted to the shot. Well-placed, it should mean instant death. A flesh wound could be crippling, but the target might be able to escape or fight in self-defense. A simple graze might knock a man unconscious, or at least leave him defenseless for a short time, while a buffalo or moose might get away.

But what about a dragon, pterosaur, whatever Gideon's quarry turned out to be?

Again, he didn't have a clue.

Against all odds, Thorn slept for ninety minutes and

woke up refreshed, dressed quickly, donned his gunbelt, and retrieved his long guns from the chifforobe. A quick stop at the water closet fixed him for the trail, and he began his walk down to the livery, conscious of townsfolk watching him along the way. *The Hieroglyph* was out by now, some of the faces that observed him showing fear and worry, others simply looking curious.

What else could he expect?

Most "normal" people wouldn't buy the story of a dragon on the loose until they saw the creature for themselves, or at the very least knew someone that they trusted who *had* seen it first-hand. A smaller number would be primed to swallow any tale, no matter how wild and outrageous, while the in-betweens would watch and wait, albeit nervously.

Thorn hoped they didn't have to meet the creature on their thoroughfare tonight, or live in dread of it for days to come.

He also hoped that no one would confuse him with Saint George.

At least he hadn't been accused, so far, of bringing trouble with him when he came to town—unless, perhaps, George Hearst might raise that charge. That struggle for New Egypt's soul was something altogether different, strictly human, and beyond the scope of Thorn's private inquiry.

People had to sort out their own woes. His province was the "Other Side," where the border between daily life and preternatural events had blurred, become obscure.

New Egypt had already crossed that line. Now Thorn was on his way to fix the problem if he could, or maybe die trying.

SIXTEEN

SILVER CROWN MINE

"Tonight you live up to your motto," Hearst told his assembled Pinkertons. "Nobody sleeps. The mine keeps operating as per usual, and every man among you stands guard duty. We can sort out giving some a rest tomorrow, when the sun's up."

Grudgingly, he had been forced into admitting that some kind of predatory creature did exist, and that it seemed to strike at night by preference. One of his own men had been taken from the Silver Crown already, and the nineteen still remaining to him—minus four dead, two recovering from gunshot wounds, and Raynard Dunn absconding like a yellow weasel—would be on alert between the hunting hours of dusk and dawn. If it returned, and Hearst half-hoped it would, massed firepower would pluck it from the sky.

His second messenger to Fort Davis had not returned with news of reinforcements yet, but they might be too late in any case,

"Be sure the Gatling's fully loaded, ready at a moment's notice," he instructed. "There's a thousand-dollar bill waiting—no, make that two, I'm feeling generous—for whoever brings down this creature, if it shows its ugly face around the mine. That's for a *single man*, mind you, and be prepared to prove your shot resulted in the kill."

Some of the Pinkertons, about one-third of them, applauded that. The others stood and stared at him, looking morose and wishing they were somewhere else. Hearst couldn't blame them, but he'd have the skin of any man who left his post and tried to slip away.

A hand went up in the back rank. "What is it?" Hearst inquired.

"Who's covering the Cornish who ain't working, sir?" a red-haired Pinkerton inquired.

"The lot of you are covering the mine and its immediate surroundings. That includes the stamp mills and the miners' bunkhouse. Clete Alford will issue individual assignments."

"Sir," another called out, "what if some of 'em try takin' off?"

"They're under binding contract," Hearst replied. "Stop them by any means required."

A couple of his shooters smiled at that, some others frowned, but none objected to the order. They were veterans of other labor battles, scattered far and wide, inured to the brutality of capital suppressing workers who forgot their place. They *were not* schooled in fighting monsters, though, and even as he spoke to them, Hearst caught some staring at the dusky sky.

"Whatever happens here tonight—and it may well be nothing—every man shall do his duty, stand his ground, and in the worst case, make his shots count. You're professionals, and I expect no less. Headquarters will be proud if you succeed, and they'll remember if you fail."

With that, he turned away, leaving the rest to Clete. When Otis Breen approached him, Hearst was lighting a cigar, his first since noon. "Well, Otis," he inquired, through drifting smoke, "you satisfied?"

"As much as can be, in the circumstances," Breen replied.

"Forget the negatives and turn your mind toward possibilities, Otis."

"And what would those be, Boss?"

"If we can kill this creature, it's a whole new source of revenue. Imagine Barnum bidding on it, or his rival, Bailey. Hell, I just might set up a museum myself, to show it off. Somewhere in the Midwest, where rubes can come from miles around, or take it on the road, whatever pays the best."

"That's optimistic," Otis said.

"I never see a glass half empty," Hearst reminded him.

"But if we fumble this, the glass could wind up broken."

"Otis, are you trying to depress me?"

"No, Boss. Sorry."

"If we have a visitor tonight, try to pitch in. I know you're not a fighter, but at times like this, all men must do their part."

"Count on it, Boss."

"Good man."

"What word from town, if you don't mind me asking?"

"Mrs. Farnum's run an 'extra' from *The Hieroglyph*, shortly before I left to come out here. I've got a copy in the trap, in case you want to read it."

"Guess I'll pass. We've had enough bad news, of late."

"In brief, its major focus is the so-called dragon, but she

still found space to rail against my speculative intervention with the Chinks and Mexicans."

"A damned shame."

"It'll come out in the wash."

"Not troubled as you were before, Boss?"

"Truth be told," Hearst said, "right now I'm spoiling for a fight."

Gideon Thorn had come back to the low hill crowned with desert willow and burr oak that hid him on his first visit to George Hearst's silver mine. With Shadow standing free behind him, farther down the rear slope, Thorn employed his spyglass, counting Pinkertons and coming up with nineteen gunmen on the property, apparently all hands on deck. Two men were stationed at the wagon-mounted Gatling gun, the other seventeen assigned to other posts.

Taking no chances, Thorn surmised. *And that's not all for me.*

Hearst had apparently decided, much as Thorn had, to be ready if the creature doubled back to any of its former hunting grounds. Barring fresh reinforcements sent from Pinkerton headquarters, he had done his best to guard the Silver Crown, its workers, and its outbuildings. Whether nineteen would be enough—or if they'd stand before the onslaught of a monster—was another question, still untested.

Part of Thorn hoped they would tough it out and do the job without him, or at least reduce his role to long-range sniping from the dark. If he was forced to show himself, approach the mine and join the fight close-in, that placed his life in double jeopardy, from Hearst's thugs and the creature he had sworn to stop at any cost.

Ideally, if the monster showed at all, Thorn would appreciate it landing, sitting still for him to place a well-aimed .50-90 bullet in its head or neck, killing it outright or disabling it and leaving what was left to the excited Pinkertons. In truth, of course, anticipating what would happen if and when the fighting started, trying to predict its outcome, was a fool's game.

Thorn had never been to war, but he remembered battling for his self-respect at Weatherford Academy in Boston, as a youngster, taking lumps at first from older boys who liked bedeviling the orphan younger kid in school, then dealing out his own once he had learned assorted native martial arts from Aunt Drusilla's African retainer and Thorn's new friend, Obi Magoro. Since then, while traveling the West, he had been forced to deal with other bullies, badmen—even one demented murderer—and some, like one of Hearst's gunmen in New Egypt, had not survived.

Killing, whether wild animals or men, had never pleased Gideon. He did not do it lightly, on a whim, but neither did he hesitate when there was no alternative.

As with a monster that devoured people randomly, at large.

Thorn watched the lookouts go about their business, some on stationary posts, others assigned to roam around the property in circuits, watching out for any threats. The night shift miners worked like those he'd seen the other day, bringing the silver ore and backfill out in rolling cars and wheelbarrows, ore bound for the stamp mills, while the detritus went into a gaping pit. Pursuit of profit turned the desert into an eviscerated moonscape, whether those who delved the earth were seeking gold or silver, copper, coal, or any other mineral that could be processed into ready cash.

At one point during Thorn's surveillance, Hearst emerged from a square hut placed near the mine's adit, a shorter, rounder figure trailing him, and spent ten minutes staring at the troops he had positioned to defend him and his interests. The guards ignored him, save for one who passed close by and raised a finger to his hat brim in a kind of half-hearted salute. Hearst nodded back and turned away, as if the Pinkerton held no personal interest for him.

Which, undoubtedly, was true.

To robber barons, workers were expendable, like checkers on a giant game board, although never crowned and turned to kings themselves. From Eastern factories to Western mines and railroad lines, from ships at see to cotton fields in Dixie, rich white men gave orders, banked the profits, while their peons of whatever race did all the scut work, suffered from the weather, blisters, broken bones, black lung and all the rest, producing wealth that they would never share.

And Thorn's own family had once been in there with the rest, immersed in shipping, whaling, and associated industries, building a fortune that could not extend their lives one day, but passed down to his maiden aunt, and finally to him, an orphan who devoted part of it to puzzling out the riddle of his early childhood.

Was he guilty, by extension, of his forebears' sins?

Perhaps, but there was nothing he could do about it now, except to wait and try to set selected problems right, one at a time.

The great winged creature is aware of hunger gnawing at its innards, and beyond that, something else it cannot name as rage but recognizes as a grave uneasiness, demanding physical response. Since its emergence from the black pit of unconsciousness, it has been searching ardently for others like itself, driven by urges built into its nature over eons when its species ruled the skies above a pristine, virgin world.

That world is gone, replaced by one acrawl with avaricious insects, swarming over arid land its memory recalls as greener and more welcoming. The sun dictates its hours now, since it is not warm-blooded in the sense that humans understand, but placed in peril by excessive heat, turned moribund by biting cold. A cave found quite by accident, among some nearby rocky peaks, protects it from the day's worst heat and after midnight, when the desert chills. If it has fed between sundown and air's swift cooling down, it sleeps in peace. If not, its stomach growls and gives it pain.

Fly south, its instinct urges, although not in words. The beast would heed it, but it has not given up on what it still vaguely recalls as home, whatever that means to a reptile thirty-odd feet long, with a wingspan exceeding forty feet. On top of that, it cannot fly far south without a full belly, the energy that it provides, its strength fully renewed after its long imprisonment.

How long?

The creature has no concept of time passing and no way to measure it. It feels *old,* but with each new feeding, more of its vitality returns. Could it be growing younger, somehow? Aging in reverse? The concept totally eludes its ten-pound brain, as do all other aspects of philosophy, science, and any other intellectual endeavor past the basics of survival.

Granted, ten pounds isn't much, within a body weighing better than five hundred pounds, and like most other animals, the creature is unconscious of the things it does not know. They don't exist for it, and never will.

But it knows how to nest, to fly, to drink and feed. What more does it require?

Tonight it turns back to the place where it first took one of the insects and some others stung it with their puny projectiles. It has already passed over the place where it fed well last night, only to find the insect hill deserted, and rejected the cramped venue of its second feeding, where a haze of noxious smoke still linkers in the air.

Back to the first one, then, and from a distance, soaring five, six hundred feet about the desert floor, it sees the fires built by its prey for light or to repel it. Once again, its brain does not process the insects' motives, only recognizing that they feed the fires deliberately, causing flames to leap and grow.

Is that a signal to the creature? Something that a larger, more evolved brain might interpret as an invitation? Or is it a warning to beware, to stay away?

It cannot grasp those notions, and the answer, if selected, would not change its course of action in the slightest. Hunger rules it now, and it must feed.

From high above the anthill, it selects a likely target and descends, flapping its great wings twice to gain momentum, then furls them against its sides to plummet like a diving falcon toward its chosen prey. It makes no warning sound except the rush of wind around its massive body as it falls.

Gideon Thorn heard nothing till the diving monster spread its wings again, to slow its downward rush a bit and keep from crashing head-on into rock and sand. The noise surprised him, a titanic popping like a giant's bedsheets flapping in a high wind on a clothesline. Glancing upward at the final instant, he beheld the monster swooping down to grab one of the Pinkertons and hoist him skyward, rising nearly out of sight.

It was too late to raise his Sharps and strive for target acquisition. There and gone, the beast might drop its mangled prey and swoop again, or carry it across the desert to New Egypt, as it had with Jed Tabor. In the first case, he would have a risky shot at best; the latter would provide no shot at all.

Clutching the Sharps, Thorn whistled softly through the dark for Shadow, probing for the stallion with his thoughts to emphasize the urgency. A moment later, hoof-beats brought him to his feet and up into the saddle, reins in his left hand, the Sharps still in his right, now elevated well above the spot where he had lain to watch the Silver Crown just seconds earlier.

From that viewpoint, eyes turned skyward, he saw the fearsome flier coming back. It circled once above Heart's property, then dropped into a spinning dive that foiled whatever hope Thorn harbored in his mind of blasting it out of the air. Below, the Pinkertons were scattering, some of them firing without really taking aim. The Gatling gun had yet to open fire, its target still too high above it for the operators of the gun to elevate their barrels adequately.

Down it came, and Slade urged Shadow down the slope to join the fight, no need on his part to demand a gallop from the gray stallion. He couldn't fire the Sharps while riding at that speed, that angle, plunging toward the flats below, but tracked the monster in its flight and also watched for any Pinkertons who might detect him, swinging toward an enemy with whom they felt more confident.

He only had two hundred yards to go before he joined them at the mine—or, rather, those who stood and fought. Some of the gunmen were already fleeing, five or six on foot, an equal number breaking for the mine's tethered remuda, sixty yards or so north of the Silver Crown's adit. Their flight reduced Hearst's fighting force to six or seven men by his count, all of them distracted at that moment by the horror swooping from the sky.

The creature grabbed a second rifleman, its talons clasped over his head and shoulders. Even in the act of climbing, huge wings beating, it still dipped its head and brought its beak to bear, ripping the Pinkerton asunder. Thorn saw one arm drop, spinning and trailing blood, and hoped the captive man had either died or passed out from the shock.

Behind the predator, Hearst's Gatling gun gave out a hollow burp of rapid fire, then instantly fell silent once again, its would-be victim rising higher, faster, than the six muzzles could elevate on their tripod. Thorn and Shadow reached the sandy flats a heartbeat later, racing toward the center of the action, where the last five Pinkertons were huddled in a ring around the Gatling's wagon, hoping that it could protect them somehow.

From the mine's mouth, Cornish workmen watched from shelter, two upholding lanterns that were hardly necessary, with the bonfires fueled by their watchdogs still burning in the open space before the mine. Their eyes were wide and white in dirt-smeared faces, all wearing expressions that revealed a state of mortal terror.

When the monster rose a second time with its dismembered victim, someone in the mineshaft shouted, "Go!" and they came streaming out, ran past the Gatling wagon and the ring of men surrounding it, sprinting toward their bunkhouse or, perhaps, the dark desert beyond. One of the Pinkertons shouted for them to stop and fired a rifle shot over their heads, but all the Cornishmen ignored him, choosing death by gunshot from behind over a dizzy flight to mutilation in the night sky overhead.

Thorn reached his destination, jumped down from his gray with Sharps in hand, and willed the stallion back to safety, slapping Shadow's rump in parting as it ran for cover in the dark behind the nearest bunkhouse. Now on foot, his rifle cocked, he searched for Hearst and failed to spot him, then divided his attention between the remaining Pinkertons and the impending death above.

SEVENTEEN

George Hearst missed Gideon completely, scuttling from Breen's shack and hoping no one saw him as he ran to reach his buggy, panting like a dog tied in the hot sun on a summer afternoon. His heart pounded against his ribs until he feared that it would burst, but what he feared more was the circling nightmare in the sky.

If asked, Hearst would have said he never panicked, but the raw emotion overtook him now, after he'd seen the monster rip some of his men apart and put the rest to flight, running like fawns and rabbits from a forest fire. It was beyond his reckoning, seen in the flesh, and all that he could think of was escape, getting away, back to The Pyramid in town and hiding in his suite till daylight.

And from there on? He had no earthly idea.

The horse that drew his trap was shying from the creature's bloody antics and the racket in the camp, struggling and neighing, but he'd hobbled it upon arrival at the mine this time and it could not escape without him. Reaching it, he struggled with the rawhide bindings for a moment, cursing his own unexpected clumsiness, then slit them with his pocket knife and threw himself into the driver's seat before the horse could recognize its freedom and escape, leaving its master in the dust.

As Hearst took up the buggy whip, he felt the Beaumont-Adams pistol's weight under his belt and almost laughed at its inadequacy. Who or *what* had he presumed to kill with that? The monster harrowing his camp was massive, seemingly immune to bullets—or, at least, the hasty shots his coward Pinkertons had fired so far—and Hearst was not about to face it on his own, with nothing but a foreign pop-gun in his hand.

An army would be needed, possibly with field artillery, if they could even sight in on a target that performed wild acrobatics in midair. It was beyond the Eye That Never Sleeps or any other gang of guns for hire that Hearst had ever dealt with, something for the true professionals.

But were there any? Who were the *professionals* at killing dragons in this day and age?

Forget it, Hearst thought, as he hauled the buggy's reins around and back toward town, fighting the sorrel's natural instinct to run as soon as its front legs had been untied. The horse fought back, in turn, but Hearst was not about to let *this* creature master him, not when he was already fleeing from a monster that could swallow both of them.

After a hectic moment when the airborne giant swooped again, tearing the right arm from another Pinkerton but somehow leaving him behind and bleeding out, Hearst managed to control the horse and aim it toward New Egypt, more or less. He then discovered that the buggy's brake was set, and he'd been wrestling with himself, as well. Cursing a blue streak in the fire-lit night, he freed it, snapped the buggy's reins, and lashed the sorrel's rump with his thin whip.

Escaping from the camp was easier than Hearst had counted on. No one obstructed him, and there was no ravenous shadow diving down to pluck him from his driver's seat. The beast was busy elsewhere, men were screaming as they ran or died, gunfire still popping off erratically, without effect. He heart the Gatling give another stutter-fart and then fall silent.

As he cleared the firelight, Hearst thought fleetingly of Otis Breen. For all he knew, his long-time mining manager was still huddled inside his squalid shack, clutching the strange Apache pistol that seemed like a toy to Hearst. The best that he could do with that against a dragon, Hearst thought, was to place the muzzle tight against his skull and pull the trigger.

Not that he wished Otis dead, but given the alternative...

When it came down to fight or flight, Hearst always leaned toward *fight*—or letting others do it for him—but there was a time to run, as well, and this was it. He fled across the desert, trailing dust that shone like silver underneath the pale three-quarter moon.

Three Pinkertons remained, one of them dying in the dust, an arm ripped off, the shoulder leaking blood now, where the crimson flow had been a torrent seconds earlier. The other two were crouched behind Hearst's Gatling gun, as if it could protect them, but the last short burst they'd fired had been a total waste, missing the monster altogether.

Gideon had recognized the germ of an idea on entering the camp, and now he tried to follow up on it, eyes sweeping his surroundings, lighting first upon a nearby shed whose door was painted with the words: EXPLO-SIVES! DANGER! That provoked a thought, but if he meant to pull it off, Thorn had to risk his own life once again, beyond what he'd already done.

He heard *Quetzalcoatl* coming, flattened on the ground, and felt its passing wind sweep over him, smelling of carrion, lifting dust devils in its wake. Thorn raised his head enough to see it make a pass over the Gatling wagon without snatching either of the last two Pinkertons still semi-functional in camp. As it flew by them, arced into a turn and climbed for elevation, both leapt from the wagon, running from the battlefield and leaving Thorn alone with what was left of their comrades.

He seized the opportunity, pushed off, and reached the wagon with its tripod-mounted meat grinder, vaulted into the bed behind the Gatling gun, and huddled there, just as the Pinkertons had done before him. Unlike them, however, Gideon possessed a strategy, however risky—even suicidal —it might seem. He hesitated to employ it but could think of nothing else to stop the flying creature here and now, *if* he could stop it, *if* it did not simply flap away before he even had the chance to try.

Movement to Thorn's right drew his eyes back toward the shack he thought must be the mine manager's on-site quarters. There, a small man was emerging from the open door, clutching a tiny pistol in one hand, his eyes behind thick glasses tracking skyward. If he noticed Thorn at all, the stranger gave no sign of it, turning away and making for the remnants of the camp's remuda in an awkward, waddling run.

No witnesses, Gideon thought, then realized that he had skipped a crucial step in his desperate plan, a key to making it succeed if he was not killed first.

Cursing, he hopped down from the wagon, Sharps rifle in hand, and ran the few yards back to the explosives shed. A simple wooden latch secured its door, easily breached, and Thorn edged into the small building, firelight guiding him, smelling a heavy scent like overripe bananas from the crates of dynamite inside.

He guessed at what he needed, set his rifle down and grabbed a dozen of the greasy sticks containing nitroglycerin and diatomaceous earth, patented as a "safe" explosive by inventor Alfred Nobel in 1867. Adding to his haul a roll of twine and twelve inches or so of fuse, Thorn heard *Quetzalcoatl* make another pass across the camp, outside, and hoped it would not be discouraged, leave the hunting ground before he had a chance to act.

I have to make it stay, he thought. A small nay-saying voice inside his head added, *Unless you're already too late.*

Rifle and dynamite in hand, he ran back to the Gatling wagon, climbed aboard, and swept the sky with anxious eyes. High up, against the moon, he saw the monster circling and he gave the Gatling's crank a wasted turn, six rounds spent to attract it with the noise and muzzle flashes if it cared to try again.

And now he had to hurry, bundling up the sticks of dynamite and tying them with twine, planting the fuse into a central stick whose detonation would explode the rest. Thorn felt a moment's panic as he wondered whether he had any matches, then removed a small box from his vest pocket and set it in the wagon's bed beside his makeshift bomb.

That done, he rose to full height, staring skyward, and removed his hat to wave it at the dragon, shouting as he did so, "Come and get me! I'm right here!"

The reptile still feels hunger, only partially assuaged. It thinks of flying back to town, now that the scuttling insects from the camp below have fled, but something sparks its dim imagination, wondering if any have concealed themselves and might be flushed from cover by another shrieking pass over the field. If so...

Down there, the loudest of their weapons flares again, winking in imitation of the larger fires around it, a staccato noise reaching the flier's ears. It cannot think of prey outsmarting it, the monarch of the skies, by setting snares. The only tricks it knows are those employed against the creatures it consumes—skimming the earth to pick them off, or plunging from on high to take them unaware. Long, long ago, when it was free to hunt in daylight, it would sometimes dive out of the gentler sun, using that light to blind its would-be meals.

Tonight, a simpler tactic should suffice. It will perform a midair roll and streak down toward the insect standing in the box with wheels, behind its weapon. When the tiny figure waves and shouts up at the sky, it means no more to the gigantic hunter than a mouse's squeaking means to any hungry owl. A bleat of fear, perhaps, or simply making noise with no reason behind it.

Feeling fresh exhilaration in anticipation of the kill, the reptile dives.

Quetzalcoatl, if that's what it was, swept down toward Gideon, a shadow first mere inches wide at altitude, then blotting out the moon and stars as it drew near. Thorn crouched behind the Gatling gun, his right hand on its crank, his left clutching a handle on the left side of its frame, behind the gun's ejection port, to swing it left, right, up, or down.

He couldn't count on any great precision work, was far from expert with the weapon, but with any luck...

The beast had leveled out, perhaps eight feet above the desert sand, coming directly at him. Thorn held his fire until it closed to twenty yards or so—an agonizing wait— then spun the Gatling's crank and kept it going, muzzles flaring, thunder pounding at his ears. Spent brass poured out the left side, clattering across the wagon's bed and bouncing off his tall black boots.

Its storm of fire seemed to surprise the dragon, which recoiled but did not flee, slowing its flight toward Thorn with giant wings outspread. He swung the Gatling back and forth, saw moonlight lancing through the half-inch holes he punched in leather wings, but couldn't tell beyond that if the concentrated fire had any great effect. The shrieking sound that issued from his would-be slayer's throat might have been pain or primal rage.

Thorn estimated that he must have fired off half the round drum magazine's supply of ammunition when the monster veered off-course and touched down to his left, one wing extended, while the other had a crumpled look about it. Was that blood smeared on its leather hide, black in the moon's glare from above?

Before he had a chance to question it, Thorn resumed firing from a range of twenty feet or so. Some of his bullets missed and kicked up spurts of sand, but others found their target, spilling more dark ichor and eliciting fresh screams that spoke of mortal agony. He thought the creature was about to die and slacked off firing, watching as it crawled across the dry earth toward the adit of the Silver Crown.

Now, when he fired, Thorn chased it, not trying to wound the creature but to *drive* it further, on and well inside the shaft. This was the ultimate denouement of his nearly hopeless plan, its penultimate moment as the injured creature clawed its way to cover, vanishing into the earth from which it had emerged eleven days before.

Thorn chased it with a final Gatling burst, .58-caliber projectiles knocking ragged divots from the Silver Crown's adit, then hopped down from the wagon with his dynamite and matches, edging toward the black pit leading underground. He heard the creature scrabbling over rock, retreating, and was forced to steel his heart against the sounds it made, almost pathetic mewling sparked by pain and vague knowledge that it had failed.

Gideon lit the fuse, clipped for a short one-minute burn, and pitched it down the shaft as far as he could manage, till its spark was out of sight but he could still hear sizzling. Back at the wagon, he retrieved his Sharps and started jogging toward the outskirts of the property, calling for Shadow with his mind.

The gray stallion appeared and stopped before him. Turning, with his left hand on its reins, Thorn felt a tremor underground and braced himself before the final *crump* of buried thunder shot a cloud of smoke and dust from the internally collapsing silver mine.

He waited for another moment, while the haze settled, wondering if the creature would reverse its track and try to bull its way through tons of shattered rock, but nothing moved inside the smoky adit. Finally, Thorn mounted Shadow and began the long, dark journey back to town.

EPILOGUE

More funerals ensued, nobody in New Egypt giving any thought to shipping home the mutilated Pinkertons, assuming that their homes could even be located. Kaiser's mortuary handled the arrangements and was paid accordingly, by Hearst, who promised that he would alert Chicago headquarters. It would be their task to inform any surviving relatives and make arrangements for the exhumation of remains should any pining relative desire return of what was left.

Gideon Thorn reckoned that there would be no takers, but who knew?

Aside from dealing with the dead, George Hearst was furious about his mine's collapse. Raging, he first blamed Thorn, then Marshal Rockwell, then the two of them together, but without a witness to support his charges, they could not proceed. His real concern was losing all the "color" trapped below, but Seth Rockwell had tried to soothe him, saying he could always hire more Cornishmen to excavate the Silver Crown's demolished shaft and start digging anew.

Before that happened, though, there was the prospect of unearthing one dead dragon, which would certainly unleash a firestorm of publicity and draw a flock of scientists to view its corpse. From there, Rockwell surmised, it was conceivable that Austin's politicians might assert control, perhaps declare the site some kind of a museum, and freeze Hearst out entirely. Rather than contend with that and spend a new fortune on bribes to head it off, Hearst left New Egypt on a stagecoach headed west, cursing the town and all within it as he headed back to California.

The big winner was Randolph Boone, who got his Chinese workers back after negotiating a small raise with Wu Chengjun and broadcast an appeal for Mexicans to work a second shift mining the mother lode. Although his mine had been the monster's seeming birthplace, no one from the state or county governments suggested that the Belle Aire should be closed for scientific research on the creature's origin.

It was a prime example of the Golden Rule—or silver, in this case. Whoever had the silver, and was willing to disperse a portion of it, made the rules.

"I still think we should dig the creature out," said Angelina Farnum, sharing Thorn's last breakfast in New Egypt at The Pyramid on Sunday morning, warm and dry July 18. "It should be studied, *analyzed*. Don't you agree?"

Thorn chewed a bite of sausage—not Aunt Lou's, she'd followed Hearst into the sunset—and replied, "I'd like to know more, personally, but the Powers That Be won't have it. Not yet, anyway. Maybe if the Belle Aire plays out."

"That could be *years* from now," she protested, face coloring. "It will be decomposed by then. We have a chance

—perhaps the only one we'll ever have—to dissect something from another age."

"Because I killed it," Thorn reminded her.

"You had no choice. The point *now* is advancing science. Don't you see?"

"I see that people will oppose you for a raft of reasons," he replied. "You know about the politics of wealth already. Silver on this scale means quick expansion for New Egypt. It'll be a boom town any time now, whether you like it or not."

"That doesn't mean—"

"And there's religion, too," he said.

"Excuse me?"

"Think about it. You've already heard the argument surrounding Darwin and his *Origin of Species*. Preachers and most politicians don't have any grasp of what he wrote. They clamor that he's saying man 'descended from the apes,' which isn't true at all. Regardless of the truth, it casts a shadow over Genesis, and now you want to scare them with a flying monster from an age some of them won't admit ever occurred? What happens to their claim that Earth's only six thousand years old as it stands today?"

"You can't be serious," she said, looking aghast.

"I'm only telling you what *they* believe, and what they'll fight for, tooth and nail. You crack their faith's foundation and you're stirring up a holy war."

"But knowledge *must* advance. You know that, more than most."

"It will," he said, "in time. But some—many—will never understand or yield to it. You'll always have a group singing 'Give Me That Old-Time Religion'."

"Jesus, Gideon."

"And then, there's fear."

"What do you mean?"

"If there was one dragon, why wouldn't there be more —or something even worse, waiting to be discovered underground, or in some jungle where the white man hasn't penetrated yet, maybe locked up in ice at the North Pole? Acknowledge one, and you admit the rest are possible. How would you ever sleep at night, for wondering and worrying?"

"I'd sleep just fine," she said. "And you?"

"I sleep all right," he answered her. " In fact, the wondering's what keeps me going."

"So you're leaving, then."

"This afternoon."

"Where are you going next?"

"Too soon to say," he said, although he *did* have several ideas. Thorn didn't want them being broadcast in a future issue of *The Hieroglyph*.

"And will you ever stop?" she asked him, almost sadly.

"Everybody stops," Thorn said. "The only question is whether you've found what you were looking for or failed."

"I hope you find out what you need to know," she said.

"I hope so, too." Raising his mug of coffee, he graced Angelina with a wistful smile. "And thanks," Gideon said.

A LOOK AT: GHOST TOWN (GIDEON THORN 3)

BY MICHAEL NEWTON

Gideon Thorn has faced down cannibals, monsters, and men possessed by evil. But nothing in his long, haunted journey has prepared him for Lazarus—a ghost town that shouldn't exist.

Fresh off a brutal case in frontier Missouri, Thorn is en route to Colorado when he interrupts a highway robbery... and is swept into the heart of a mystery deeper than any before. Stranded on the Kansas prairie, he and a handful of strangers are welcomed as "guests of honor" by the unnervingly polite citizens of Lazarus—a settlement thought destroyed during a Confederate raid years ago.

But something is terribly wrong. The town is frozen in time. Its inhabitants harbor unsettling secrets. And as the anniversary of its fiery razing approaches, Thorn must uncover the truth behind Lazarus before its curse consumes them all.

In a land steeped in blood and shadow, Thorn's quest for answers may end where the dead refuse to rest.

AVAILABLE NOVEMBER 2025

ABOUT THE AUTHOR

A California native, Michael Newton published over 215 books under his own name and various pseudonyms since 1977. He began writing professionally as a "ghost" for author Don Pendleton on the best-selling Executioner series. With 104 episodes published to date, Newton nearly tripled the number of Mack Bolan novels completed by creator Pendleton himself.